Mean Streets Echo

A Peggy d'Sousa Mystery

Sue Neacy

iUniverse, Inc.
New York   Bloomington

iUniverse books may be ordered through booksellers or by contacting:

iUniverse
1663 Liberty Drive
Bloomington, IN 47403
www.iuniverse.com
1-800-Authors (1-800-288-4677)

ISBN: 978-1-4502-1641-8 (sc)
ISBN: 978-1-4502-1642-5 (ebook)

Printed in the United States of America

iUniverse rev. date: 03/05/2010

Contents

CHAPTER I

One Cold Night

Shadowy empty streets gave me the feeling I was the only person left in the world. Even the panhandlers had more sense than to be out on this freezing winter's night. An exceptional blast of icy wind hit me as I turned onto Van Ness off Geary. I stopped to pull my coat collar up above my ears, zipping it.

An SFPD car cruised by on patrol, colored lights eerie in the night. Hard to believe what happened next.

A lone figure stepped into the middle of the road. Streetlights behind cast such a massive shadow they made him look like a giant. He threw back his head and let out a thunderous roar of laughter, lifted a shotgun and fired at the cop car's windshield.

The driver didn't stand a chance, slumping dead over the wheel. The car, clipping along, slewed across the road into the nearest light pole. Its siren began a mournful wail. Worse, flames began licking underneath.

I ran to it in panic to help the other cop, who was vainly trying to crawl from the passenger side. I think both her legs were broken. The door was so crumpled there's no way we could get it open. I hammered on the widow to break it. Hopeless! It needed something solid. I mouthed the words "your gun," through the window. The cop understood, grabbed her gun and smashed the window with the butt.

I was able to drag her through the broken glass to get her

out. Despite the pain and the blood this caused, both of us were desperately conscious of the ever encroaching fire.

Above the cacophony of the dying car, the injured cop's moans, I heard the ratchet of the monster re-arming his shotgun. I snatched the cop's gun, fired blindly in hope.

He fell backwards onto the road. Out of the light his size diminished to that of a normal human. Behind him shadows faded as he fell. I sensed a wolf pack that retreated without its leader.

Better keep the gun out.

The car suddenly went up with a roar of sound. Feeling the sudden heat of searing flame, I tugged the injured cop further away. I could see her eyes starting to fade. Talk, Peggy, talk…

"Bloody hell! First time I've been warm since I hit this town!"

She came back to life, gave me a weak smile.

"We need help, and quick!"

She indicated her top pocket. I pulled out her cell phone, went to dial the Aussie emergency 000 then remembered it wouldn't get me far in San Francisco. I hesitated. What was it? "911 is the emergency number?"

"Here." Weak as she was, she took the phone off me and hit an emergency button. "Officer Taylor…" She reported the incident in the string of gobbledegook numbers cops use. I only comprehended 'Intersection of Geary and Van Ness.' Then she tucked the phone away and looked around, suddenly seeing the burning car, the figure being enveloped by flames slumped over the wheel. Instinctively she tried to force herself to her feet and go to him, sobbing and gasping, "Chuck…Chuck…"

Cradling her, I pressed her face close to me, shielding her from the horrific sight of her partner burning to a crisp.

"Chuck was dead before you hit the pole. He isn't feeling anything."

She fell back with a low moan as the stench of burning flesh filled the air. I crouched over her with gun at the ready against who knows what, until the alarms and sirens cutting through the night drew near, then tucked the gun back into her holster.

Paramedics reached the scene first, then about ten police cars. In the mayhem, the first cop car to arrive almost ran over the Monster's body on the road. They loaded Taylor into an ambulance, reporting to one of the cops as we stood stamping our feet in the cold.

"Yes, I saw everything. Was walking back to my hotel - the Ramada on Market…"

That's as far as I got before crumpling to the ground, covered in Taylor's blood and gore.

CHAPTER 2

Oil and Water

There was an inevitability about it.

The moment I looked into Charlie Deakins' eyes, the sudden bolt of electricity that passed between us guaranteed that I would wake up naked in Charlie's bed.

I'd only met Charlie a few hours earlier in the SFPD Police Superintendent's office, where I'd swished in wearing my best grey wool suit. The message at the hotel had "requested my presence" at SFPD Headquarters at 9am. Given that the hospital had just let me go, arriving about noon at the hotel I was lucky to get there that same day.

Surprisingly, I was instantly ushered into some high level cop's office, not an interview room.

Charlie had opened the door. "Ah, Ms. Marguerite d'Sousa I presume?" He winked and retreated to the shadows. Superintendent Clarke, all braid and very official snarled grumpily "d'Sousa? The damn Private Eye? You're late!" He then reached into a drawer and pulled out a piece of paper.

"What's this?"

"Your check for one million dollars." He grated the amount out through clenched teeth. "As you would know very well, there was a bounty for a million dollars on the head of Michael James Hewitt, otherwise known as The Enforcer."

"Wow!" I held up my hand. "As I *did not know* Superintendent.

I've been in this city less than a week. You're talking about the guy I shot the other night, the Monster?"

The uniformed cop gave me a look of absolute disbelief. "Monster? Good name for him. After he finished twenty years in prison, he vowed to get as many police officers as possible. Charles Timms was number eight."

"Charles…Chuck…the driver of the patrol car the other night?"

"Yeah."

"And did Officer Timms leave a family?"

"Wife and five kids."

"And what about Officer Taylor, how is she? Going to need a lot of expensive medical?"

"Yeah. She'll need a lot of hospital care, but she'll get there. She's supporting a couple of kids…no husband."

I folded my arms. "You got collections going for both these guys?"

"Of course."

I pulled out my personal checkbook, writing out checks for $500,000 each for the widow and the injured Thompson.

"Don't worry, I'm good for it even before I put this," I waved the reward check over my head, "In my account. Now, I want to make sure that the SFPD has on record my report about the others who were there with the Enforcer that night…"

"We have that covered, Ms. d'Sousa." The Superintendent wasn't going to keep a PI in the police station longer than he had to – enough that he had given me $1,000,000.

"I'll, er…see you home," grinned Charlie, grabbing my arm and steering my out of the office, laughing out loud as we hurried down the corridor.

"He was all dressed up for a television shot and you were a no-show."

"I was in hospital!" I snarled indignantly.

I let Charlie lead me downstairs to the car park.

"Your place or mine?" he asked in the car.

"Yours." I had already forgotten the braided superintendent, shooting covert looks at my driver.

Charlie was five feet three inches of solid muscle from the top of his head to his toes, no neck to speak of and a ruddy, weather-beaten face, topped with a wisp of sandy hair and strange, tiger-like eyes.

He looked as if he should be wearing a beret and jumping out of planes in foreign parts, not pretending to be a policeman.

That said, he was undoubtedly the most sensual man on the planet.

A couple of hours later he rolled over in bed and said: "I want to make you a proposition."

"I thought we were well past that scenario."

He swung out of bed, pulled on a very modern prosthetic leg before slipping into a lairy pair of silken USA flag boxer undies. He sashayed without even the suggestion of a limp across the enormous penthouse bedroom to an oversized video.

"What's so funny?"

"Dammit, Charlie. You look like Central Casting's idea of a parachute major. I'm right, aren't I?"

"Yeah, well, blokes who jump from planes shouldn't land on mines," he admitted.

"Very careless," I agreed.

He came and lay back beside me, hugging me in his great muscular arms, before flicking the remote and bringing the big screen in front of us to life.

"I like that. No sloppy sentimentality…just noting facts about people. That's professional. Thing is, you get hurt – you get on with it. It's the job. So now please watch the damn screen, then we'll talk."

Immediately evident was that it was the security vid from a massive shopping centre, this camera focussed on the busy main escalator…one of the longest I'd ever seen.

Suddenly a terrified looking woman stumbled into view, forcing her way onto the crowded moving stairs. Shoving annoyed people aside in her haste she clawed her way upwards. Stymied at last, forced to stand still, she flung one fearful glance down. A shot rang out. She dropped dead.

Charlie pressed the stop button.

"That was some dead-eye shooting… moving target, distance,

split second of time to fire. We weren't – and still are not – 100% sure it's even the right vic.

"Homeland Security has to look at all cases of 'single shot' murders…or in your case, self defence. Things like one-off pistol shots from an extreme distance. Seems you have a history," he said accusingly.

"Do I take it you are referring to my shooting of the drug lord in Perth, 2005?"

"Yeah. I gather circumstances were very similar to your shooting the other night – more self-defence than anything. Even so, the Police Super is convinced you are some kind of bounty hunter. To his mind, nobody brings down a man with a million dollar bounty on his head with a lucky shot!"

"Cops and PI's – oil and water."

I hit the remote. "Too many unanswered questions. Why was she running? How did the gunman know where to wait? Aha, there he is. That's why. He chased her until she hit the escalator, then coolly stood to one side, pulled out the gun, aimed it at her head and waited for a clear shot. See the shadow at the bottom of the stair? Should even show a flash from there." I re-wound and replayed the tape. It did.

Charlie swore. "All the bozos who missed the obvious. So much for experts!"

"Too easy. So I'd say definitely the right vic. But who was she?" I had a very strong feeling of having seen that face before.

"One Mrs Candy-Jane Dickerson, a prominent Chicago citizen. It was opening day of a new shopping centre in Chicago in which she had a serious investment."

The name meant nothing so I kept talking, trying to shake some half-memory free. "So I'm guessing everyone from the other shopping centre investors, to the mayor, to the governor all want answers and want them quick… hence you, America's chief trouble-shooter, have been called in?"

The wry smile that accompanied that work description suggested I'd nailed him pretty closely as a specialist "trouble shooter". Mark up a couple of brownie points to Peggy.

"OK, so don't tell me who you really are." I re-ran the video, freezing it just before the shooting.

"I never forget a face Charlie and I've seen that one before. But where? Of course! A Gendarme pointed her out to me. South of France – a bloody long time ago. If I'm right, I've news for you boyo. That aint Candy-Jane Dickerson. Her name is Conseula Carpentier, the daughter of one Mitch Carpentier, head of the tough Marseilles boys of whom said gendarme reported: 'zey are not nice people'.

"Hang on…got something on my files back home." It was my turn to pad naked across the bedroom, drawing a whistle from Charlie, wriggling my hips suggestively as I bent down and searched for my mini laptop inside my big handbag. I meandered back to the bed and propped myself up on pillows.

I soon had the connection that allowed me to get into my files at home.

"Ah – Conseula Carpentier." I pulled up the picture. "Taken then with the hidden mini camera in my handbag. Always carry it - just in case."

"I'll remember that." Then he concentrated on the photo on my screen. "Could be. Old photo but could be."

"Is, Charlie, admit it."

Then I scanned through info I'd put onto the file over time as a matter of course. "Let's see, rumour has it Conseula ran off with one Henri Dressant, Carpentier's chief lieutenant. For a wedding gift they helped themselves to a truckload of daddy's heroin.

"Not surprisingly, Henri washed up in the Seine with a single bullet between his eyes a couple of years later, almost certainly killed by…killed by…"

My voice trailed away. "The Lone bloody Wolf." I clicked off my computer and whistled. "So that's what **you** are **really** all about! Did the bullet in Conseula match?"

He nodded. "We didn't get what he was doing back here, or why he killed some sweet innocent Chicago matron. With what you've just told me, it suddenly makes sense."

"Always one shot, always from the same gun."

I shook my head. The Lone Wolf was a world wide legend – had been for twenty years.

Charlie smiled bewitchingly, crossed his arms. "To know all this, who are *you* really?"

"Marguerite d'Sousa, Private Investigator…and as the good Superintendent Clarke of the SFPD would never admit, a good PI is always two steps ahead of the cops – mostly because of this." I shook my computer.

Charlie bellowed with laughter. "Well, I'm hoping that is so because I want to pick your brains. You've already told me more than I've learned in a year of looking with a top team over in Langley…"

"I thought Langley was CIA?" I picked that up quickly.

"Yeah, well…"

"Fact is, who are *you* really?"

"I thought maybe you could help us, offer some ideas outside the square, so to speak."

"So *that's* why you've been romancing me?"

We snuggled some more.

"What do you say?"

I'd been too long away from the streets. I was bored and hungry for action. Besides, this wasn't just action, it was the *Lone Wolf*. I tried to look cool, calm and professional. "I'd say I need to look at all CIA files on the Lone Wolf, see if I can come up with a different angle."

"Understood." He swung off the bed.

"Oh, and one last thing. I cost."

"Understood." He laughed loudly. "Anyone who can toss away a million dollars without a blink must have made a pot out of security."

"Now Charlie, I am insulted. If you knew me better, you'd know I'd have split that reward money into the police victims' funds even if my bank balance was zero."

He stood and looked at me. "Darlin', I believe you. Don't know if the SFPD will though."

"Talking of the SFPD, can you drop me off at the hospital. I want to visit Thompson – and I need to get her some flowers."

He laughed. "The lift I can give you. Flowers she won't need."

CHAPTER 3

Lefty Four Eyes

I could see what Charlie meant as I forced my way down the hospital corridor into Taylor's private room through a floral jungle. She had both legs wrapped in plaster and suspended, as well as both arms heavily bandaged where she had copped deep gouges from glass from the windshield and then the side window.

"At least I managed to protect my face," she said with a proud grin.

"You are one amazing dame to have got yourself out of that car, then dialed for help!"

"**You** are a puzzle – shoot like a dream but don't even know the 911 code! I told Charlie here I thought you were a foreigner. You ended up in emergency too?"

"Guilty on both counts. I looked a sight and was rushed to emergency! Having got me there they stuck some pills in me and I woke up 36 hours later.

"The Police Superintendent was miffed I didn't show on time for some TV doorstep thing he put his best uniform on for. Never occurred to him to enquire after my health.

"Didn't help that I'm a PI. Name's Peggy. I'm from Western Australia – it's sort of the California of Oz, only we have warmer weather, real sandy beaches and lots of surf. You should get there some time for a holiday. How are your kids going?"

"Loving being celebrities in class. They're old enough to handle themselves at home alone for a while. Thanks for that dough, we'll need it."

"Check out the difference in pay between Oz and here – the local cops are always trying to recruit anyone with a police background."

"You know, I just might do that."

Satisfied that Taylor was getting the 'royal' treatment – at least for the time being – I left with Charlie, who was laughing again.

"What's so funny?"

"You go there just to recruit her?"

"Damn, I just bet you got there first?"

"You bet!"

Someone I didn't have to worry about anymore.

Charlie took me back to his apartment, dug out the spare keys and showed me how to dial into his computer to get all the facts on Lone Wolf.

"Sorry Peggs, gotta rush. Here's my card and phone number if you need me in a hurry."

The Guggenheim & Guggenheim security job that had brought me to San Francisco had been finished the night of the shooting. I dropped into their new office opening party, checked on all the security equipment and was polite to all the heavies since they were my bread and butter - a global jewellery company based out of Amsterdam, who paid well and quickly.

Formalities completed and with money on my mind, I called into the bank, paid in the million dollar check telling them to ring the Police Commissioner if it worried them. To be fair, they acted as if it were a normal daily transaction. While there I drew out a wad of play money and headed out for a musical that night.

Late night after the show I deliberately walked the mean streets back to the Ramada. Lots of things were still bugging me. It was cold, yet the usual panhandlers were out on the streets this night. One I had done business with before.

"Hey Jimmy."

"Yo!"

I pulled a ten dollar note out.

"Too cold for everyone on the street the night that cop was killed?"

"Meanin'?"

"The streets were empty. Someone drop the word to stay clear? I need a name."

"Harry the Hook." He snatched at the ten dollar note laughing, then trundled his trolley away, stopping to call over his shoulder: "Hope youse is carrying. Harry's quick on the draw."

I sensed rather than knew Harry was up back of me somewhere and had given the nod for Jimmy to talk.

"I'm carrying too," I said to the air, pulling a roll of hundreds out of my pocket.

Harry came up behind me, patting me down for a gun. He took the notes and counted. "I aint no snitch."

"No. And I aint no cop. Got any good ideas about who would have been with the Enforcer that night?"

"Well, ole Lefty Four Eyes is a San Franciscan – likely he was there."

"You're putting me on. 'Lefty' because he's left handed and 'Four Eyes' because he wears glasses, right?"

Harry chuckled maliciously. "Almost. Don't have no right hand. Used to call hisself the Enforcer's *left* hand man." He cackled. "Know how he lost the hand?"

"The Enforcer?"

"Yep. Stole something off 'im in prison. Enforcer chopped his right hand off. Said he'd do the same to anyone else."

"And Lefty ended up working with him?" I was incredulous.

"Once you know who's boss and who aint, you got a good partnership going, right?"

"Yeah."

I repeated this conversation to Officer Taylor in the hospital the next day. She didn't say anything, but she had obviously heard of both Harry and Lefty.

"No one in the SFPD is going to listen to a PI – especially one who ruined the Superintendent's chance to make the six o'clock news. Do with this information what you want. Ball is in your court. My gut feeling was there was a wolf pack out there behind the Enforcer whilst we were lying on the ground. What worries me is they are still out there. They also know how to shoot cops."

"For a PI, you're OK," she cracked back.

Time to take on Charlie's problem. I buried myself in work, spending the next couple of days and nights at Charlie's place, going through the files on the Lone Wolf. Then I put it to one side.

Heck, I'd taken the San Francisco security job because I loved this quirky city and its people. There were all sorts of fascinating layers of good and bad.

I started at the top as pure tourist, riding the cable cars to the Wharf where I ate far too much, so worked it off by standing in the queue that got me on the ferry to Sausalito.

Then I couldn't resist heading out with other wide eyed tourists on a "see San Francisco trip", marvelling at the "painted ladies" in the city, the astounding redwoods of Muir Woods, where quiet deer peered from behind trees at you with big sad brown eyes then ran off startled, whereas noisy sea lions welcomed you back at Fisherman's Wharf clamouring for attention.

Things had begun to gel inside my head by the end of the week when Charlie rang.

"You free for a seafood dinner tonight?"

"Can do."

We sat overlooking the Bay in a discreet, expensive restaurant. Clearly Charlie hadn't brought me here for romance. We both ordered the biggest seafood platter on the menu. As soon as these were delivered he fixed me with a questioning gaze.

In between peeling and munching prawns I outlined theories. "The main point is: Unlike the almost laughably unprofessional so-called terrorists around the world (including Al Quaida), the Lone Wolf knows who is 'listening' to email and fax chatter and ducks 'under the radar' of Langley types by *never* using emails or a mobile phone."

Charlie nodded agreement and frustration.

"Next: the dead people are all gangsters. This is someone who has a brilliant understanding of the dynamic of underworld gangs, especially who is in, who is on their way up. That kind of specialist knowledge suggests an insider – either of the gangs or whose job is to monitor the bad guys."

"Meanin'?"

"Someone in some branch of law enforcement."

Charlie snorted his derision.

I shrugged and pulled another prawn to pieces.

"I can't work out how contact is being made to hire the Assassin. I just don't have a clue. However, the first law of being a Private Eye is follow the money. So how is Lone Wolf paid? Certainly not by electronic bank payment you guys can pick up.

"The records show this person is the best assassin in the world. That must mean seriously **big** money. Payment must be made by some other means than hard cash.

"I've kicked some ideas around. The one I like best is with a genuine piece of art. It's easy to carry and the Lone Wolf can off-load at leisure. I'm certain therein lies the weakness. There we will find him or her."

Charlie halted in mid-bite. "You seriously believe the Lone Wolf could be a 'her'?"

"It struck me it's the sort of gun I would choose …lightweight, reliable."

"Genteel, upper crust?" he sneered.

"Unlikely. Look at the list of victims. All hard nosed gang members. We're talking about someone who is streetwise enough to know the inner workings of half a dozen gangs in the US, professional enough not to change to political targets.

"The victims were probably threats to gang leaders or were even taking over someone's patch. In many ways the Lone Wolf was helping society by getting rid of evil types the cops just couldn't keep behind bars.

"Now I've done enough talking. Do you have any more you can tell me?"

There had been about Charlie's sudden exit after a call on his cell phone the suggestion that new evidence had come to light.

We paused as the empty seafood platters were whipped away and we dickered over deserts and coffee. At last Charlie opened up.

"Good guess. We now know the famous gun was one of many used in a school massacre a few years before the first Lone Wolf murder."

"Aha! Whereabouts?"

"Chicago. Apparently, Police and FBI computers were being upgraded at the same time, so by sheer luck the CIA was sent the bullet because we had the only means to do nationwide matchups.

"I say 'luck' because although we are positive the information was later transferred to the new Police and FBI files, it is no longer there… hence the time we have taken to come up with this background.

"The bad news is that the relevant Chicago PD handling the case has since closed and moved. All the guns confiscated at the time of the massacre have gone missing. My guess, sadly the most obvious is that they hit the streets and were sold off. It's a cold trail."

"Cold? Oh come off it Charlie! Haven't you been listening to single word I said?

"You've just told me upgraded FBI and PD computers have been tampered with. It fits perfectly with my profile. Surely it's more likely that one of Chicago's best and finest decided plodding around in the rain and snow was a high risk no future occupation and secured one of the guns with ammo…then covered their tracks?"

"A cop? This isn't just some anti-cop kick you're on, being a PI?"

All the evidence I'd put before him after studying the files, I couldn't believe he had the same knee-jerk reaction as the police superintendent. I was rightly furious and slammed my hand hard down on the table. Diners around us looked up. We called for more coffee and waited 'til the coast was clear before I carried on.

"It makes so much sense. Think about it. Anyone…" I paused for breath "Anyone with a few years on the job at a tough PD would know all there was to know about gangs and how they worked. They'd be savvy about who was doing what to who from word on the street. They'd also be a sharp shooter, not to mention well trained on police department computers and clear that you lot would be listening in to any computer or phone chatter."

He held up his hands. "OK, OK! I'll buy that it's *possible*."

"More than…"

"Any suggestions on how move forward from here." Charlie spoke softly, trying to recover his cool.

This was the hard bit, because I really wasn't one hundred percent sure in my own heart. "Give me the case. Give me my head." I still had a lot of scars from my last case, but this felt right.

"Go after the Lone Wolf yourself?" Charlie was shaking his head. He was still protesting as we reached his apartment after dinner.

"Softening me up?" he whispered.

"Damn right, Deakins."

We lay in bed arguing over the case half the night, in between making love. Crazy! By morning he had come around to my point of view.

"OK. I give in. The case is yours alone. I give you back-up. What do you need?"

"It all points to Chicago. I'll need to sight Chicago cops back employment files for the period of the shooting and the office changeover – the original paper files, not those on computer. Computer records are absolutely no good to us if these have been messed with. *We* have to learn not to use the computer as well."

Charlie whistled. "Old records will take time to trace and even then it could take forever!"

"Time I've got. Incidentally, I want a written contract…which includes today!"

"I must be crazy," he muttered.

No, I was, for talking myself into the job.

CHAPTER 4

Chicago

The contract when it arrived was more than generous. Included were all the security passes I might need plus an address in Chicago where all the old papers were stored. I would have to go to them, because of a major problem.

The "problem" was easy. The big chill had settled across north America and Chicago in particular. It was snowed in. No planes were getting in or out. Two days later, suitably padded up with chill-proof clothing, I boarded an Amtrak train and headed east.

Despite the rough weather, the trains were getting through. Amtrak delivered me only a couple of hours late, from where I took the EL to a slightly obscure station towards the Loop.

That was the easy bit. I was booked in to a hotel across the road from the old Hall of Records, "not far" from the station.

Once at ground level, I battled the blizzard, setting off on foot into the teeth of the howling wind and driving snow to my destination.

I didn't dare stop. I fell over a lot. Exhaustion and frostbite had set in to my whole body by the time I arrived at the hotel. At first I almost didn't get through the door, let alone take up my booked and prepaid room, the night clerk pleading all the excuses hotels think up when they've let your room out to someone else.

I had just come from the North Pole. Nothing impressed me. A room with heating NOW was my minimum demand. We almost came to a fistfight at the entrance.

The Manager came out to see what the disturbance was all about.

He owned I must be the "special guest" to be given "all consideration" they had been waiting for (someone had apparently forgotten to tell the night clerk these small facts).

Magically my room appeared vacant on their booking screens. The Manager personally led me to this. I threw him out and collapsed on the bed…after first checking the heating.

I think I slept for 12 hours solid out of pure exhaustion. Then I woke up bruised, battered and hungry. I tried to get an idea of where I was from my hotel window. It was filthy. Outside was darkish and looked over an alley way. "Room with a view" as they say. I was filled with a sense of old fashioned down town buildings, as I bundled myself into my blizzard breaking clothes and headed for the exit. I walked out into crisp, clear sunlight that made me blink. The blizzard had blown itself out overnight, leaving behind surprisingly little ice and snow. Down the road the lights of 'Kim's Diner' beckoned.

I stepped inside. It was a huge, barn-like yet somehow comfortable place, filled to the brim with hungry Chicago-ites, accustomed to taking the early EL to work and eating breakfast at Kim's on the way.

You could see why. The board listed all those massive breakfasts for which America was once famous and I ordered a "Super Kims". As I stood at the counter defrosting, two men came in. I suddenly realised they weren't wearing balaclavas against the cold. Each was brandishing a shotgun.

"Git-down everyone. Hit the floor. This is a hold up!" They screamed. The noisy place went quiet, then pandemonium struck as people dove under tables.

I was seriously pissed off and very hungry. I hurled myself at the pair, slammed their heads together, kicked them in the "family jewels" and relieved them of their guns.

"Hey Kim," I called over the counter to the crouching owner. "Put these in a safe place, give me something to tie these idiots up with, call the cops – but first *get me my breakfast*!"

People clambered back to their feet and sat down again. As my breakfast arrived, an idea was half forming in my head. I could have been out of there before the cops arrived. I decided to keep eating, slowly. Finally a cop came over to me and grabbed me by the arm.

"Ma'am, we're going to have to take you up town to take your statement."

"Son, I aint going anywhere before I finish my breakfast – and you can shoot me if you like, but that's a solid fact."

Kim was talking to the media by now. The bad guys were hauled out. I left with the cops. Everyone in the diner stood up and clapped. I made sure the cameras got my good side as we hit the paparazzi scrimmage.

When I got to police HQ, I was asked what I was doing in the US. I produced Charlie's card and said I was assisting this gentleman. Eventually they rang him. I went from hard bench downstairs with the bad guys, to upstairs front office with a view and the top cop.

"Sorry Ma'am. Thanks for your help today."

The boys from the PD gave me a lift back to my hotel but it was already too late to do any work that day. I went down to 'Kim's Diner' and got a decent free dinner on the house and an early night.

The next day I crossed the road to the Hall of Records. Seems like everyone there had seen me on the telly news or read about me in the paper. I was the famous "Aussie who saved 'Kim's Diner'," their favourite local haunt, so they took me to their hearts.

I explained that before looking at any records, I needed to talk to someone with a good background of happenings in Chicago many years ago. I was hoping to find someone like that working there, but was out of luck. However, the huge African American guy with a limp who manned the desk thought for a while.

"What youse needs is Evangeline."

Evangeline had worked at the Hall of Records most of her life and retired two years before. She didn't live far away and someone came up with her current address.

This old lady lived in a walk up brownstone just around the corner. "It may be old," she wheezed as she opened the door, "but even in this weather, the damn plumbing still works. I got heating."

Heating was important to a lady both of whose hands were crippled with arthritis. She pulled me inside and sat me down in the only spare chair, fussing in a way that suggested guests were too rare these days. She said Harley had rung and warned I'd be on my way and told her what I wanted.

I asked her did she remember a school shooting in Chicago going back nearly thirty years.

"Oh my yes. It was Public School Number 5, just down the road. We were shocked, although we're pretty tough around here." Coming from a wisp of a woman, this made me laugh. "What I mean is, we were used to gangsters and gangs, but the school shooting – that was something altogether new. It shook us all."

"A sign of the changing times?"

"I'm afraid so."

"Can you remember anything about it?"

"Feller called Pil...Powcheski – that's it. Powcheski. He was tough, in one of them Polak gangs. Didn't get on with the Brothers. He always reckoned the Brothers' mob raped his sister, so he come to school and shot 'em. Said a man had to do what a man had to do. He was 13 years old!"

"And had the Brothers' gang raped his sister?"

"No. Seems the two groups used to call out bad stuff to each other and their relatives across the streets - you know how kids' gangs are. It was all words but she got upset and embellished it by the time she got home. He got it wrong. Now he's on death row. Been there all his life."

"That's the saddest thing I ever heard. How many people did he shoot?"

"Fifteen."

"*Fifteen!* He must have been carrying an arsenal!"

"Funny thing, in some ways the whole neighbourhood settled down after that. People started being nice to each other…"

"But fifteen dead isn't a shooting, it's a war!"

"Yeah!"

She told me the dates of the incident. Then I asked her whether she knew anything about the old PD closing.

"That's where the Hall of Records is now. Reckoned that opened in mid March of 1975."

"So the police station I went to yesterday was opened then and the cops moved uptown?"

"Yeah."

"Must have been pretty tough being a cop in those days?"

"Aint that the truth. They were caught between the two. Harley at the front desk now – he's an ex-cop. The Polak gang shot him just for being black."

"And your husband," I asked softly, pointing to photo.

"You got good eyes. Never did find out who, but swings and roundabouts - I guess it could even have been one of the boys killed in the Public School shooting."

No wonder those times were still vivid to her. Her hands would never have enabled her to hold a gun, but I didn't doubt if she'd ever found out who really killed her husband, she might have had a go.

"You have any family?"

"Growed up, moved away. But I'm a Chicago gal through and through. They give me a job at the records hall after Brian, when an…"

"Least they could do."

The old lady wiped a tear. "Long time ago."

"Evangeline, you have been a huge help. Is there anything I can do for you?"

Her eyes twinkled. "Surely. Drop by one Friday with a Kim's Special breakfast and help me eat it!"

"You got it!"

My cell phone rang. It was Charlie, almost beside himself with rage. "You're supposed to be there incognito, Peggy! Now I turn on my TV and see you!"

"Charlie, when you're in private industry, you learn a little publicity is never, ever a bad thing."

He hung up with a muttered curse.

CHAPTER 5

Running Scared

Next morning I found myself surrounded by ancient, musty, and very dusty files at the Hall of Records.

How would I know who I was looking for from all these? The sheer span of murders required she or he be young when they started as the Lone Wolf. Not a complete rookie, but one experienced on the street and on computers. I was inclined towards a woman – although there wouldn't have been too many women on the force in those days. Certainly it would be someone in uniform. The strange fact of the bullet being forwarded on to Langley at the time of the school massacre would have been well known by the homicide detectives. However, whoever altered the Police and FBI records didn't know. It narrowed down the start time to about 1974.

There was a high turnover. Too many cops had retired hurt, or had died on duty. The place must have been like a war zone. I spent hours browsing musty old files before one jumped out at me. The profile fitted. The photo was of a female officer. What the cops call a "definite maybe". Everything fitted.

I picked up my cell phone, dialed Charlie.

"I think I've found Lone Wolf…" then I stopped. That old gut feeling I hadn't felt for years hit me strongly. "Don't trust this mobile. I'm heading for the station pay phones. Ring you back."

I looked to left and right as I left the building – not a car in sight. Maybe I was being paranoid. These days it was easy peasy to just sit in your car and pick up vision from interiors on a hand held cam…

let alone monitor a mobile. Even so I back-trekked around the block to make sure I wasn't followed.

At the EL station, I found a bank of phones and rang again. "Ring me back immediately on a secure phone on this number, Charlie."

It seemed an age as I stood there, my finger on the depress, waiting for the return call.

"Stop playing games, Peggy. What have you got?"

"Name, Miriam Dupont, beat cop in the Chicago PD. There's thirty years of change, but I think…mind you…only *think*…"

All the time I talked, I'd been switched on, glancing around, my nervous antenna beeping like mad. Something was wrong. I caught the smallest of movements and jerked. There was an amazing noise. My neck hurt. The pay phone exploded as if in slow motion as a bullet hit where my head had been a split second before. I hit the ground fast, rolling.

I tossed my cell phone under an incoming train then jumped aboard. I hung my scarf around my neck to hide the area blood was coming from.

When I hit Union I found a toilet, tried to wash the blood away and stem the wound. With my snow jacket turned inside out, wearing it around my shoulders, I looked almost normal.

I got a sleeper to San Francisco, that got me out of there fast.

To say that I didn't feel good by the time I arrived was putting it mildly. I staggered out of my cab in the dark, checking back into the Ramada.

Before heading for the rooms, I went to Joe, one of the night shift staff I recognised, offering him a fifty. Insulted he waved it away.

"Joe, do you know of a doctor can patch people up no questions asked? I'm in room 504."

He gave me a hard look. "*He'll* need five big ones."

"Understood." I handed over the cash.

A discreet knock came on the door about twenty minutes later. The elderly retired gent seemed to know what he was doing. He sat me down in the bathroom, cleaned the wound. "The bullet went straight through. You're lucky. If it was the other side of your neck it would have hit the main artery. Even so, you've lost way too much blood. You aren't a drug runner or anything?"

I smiled weakly. "No, I'm one of the good guys."

"So Joe said. I trust his judgement."

Next morning I bought some new clothes, unbloodied, went back to the hotel to shower and dump the old, then feeling almost new walked into Chinatown.

The speed Lone Wolf had reached me in Chicago suggested that – like Evangeline, Lone Wolf hung close to home. Maybe not all the time, but enough. My bad luck to have been there when she was. My first impulse was to return to Chicago.

However, I knew I hadn't been followed from the Hall of Records. Someone had overheard my cell phone conversation. Instinct told me the Lone Wolf might never use a cell phone or email, but was into serious hi-tech tracking. That was my game. Almost as a matter of honour, I needed to be ahead of the other player.

I called on Jimmy Wong…more in hope than expectation. He shook his head. I knew what he was going to say next. "Hong Kong only place for that."

There were many container ships that carried passengers. Hong Kong by sea was going to waste time, but was safer.

Decision made, I had a last meal at Fisherman's Wharf then trekked back to the hospital, where I paid a visit to Officer Taylor.

"You look like shit!"

"I've been better. I need your help."

"Shoot."

"Remember that other recruiting guy…?"

"Charlie? Sure."

"He leave you a number to call, or…"

"No. Said he'd get back to me."

"Yeah, that's what I thought likely. Give it a couple of days. If you haven't heard from him, ring him on this number and tell him you've seen me."

"That's it?"

"Yeah."

"Peggy – duck next time." She sounded anxious.

"Best advice I've had in a week!"

We both laughed.

As I checked out of the Ramada the cheeky desk clerk asked: "Should we keep your room for you Ma'am?"

I grabbed the duffle bag I'd bought that day and headed off for the wharf where I boarded the *Reliance,* which buffeted its way into the Pacific Ocean that night.

The very first night at sea, the nightmare, the bad case that had caused me to give up detecting and turn to security, came back to haunt me:

Beanie shimmered on from nowhere just as the doors were about to close. As always she chose the lead carriage. A wraith, more skeleton than flesh, it was the beanie on her head that had caused me to give her the nickname. I'd followed it through the back alleys and dark places of Fremantle for the last ten days. Red, woollen, scruffy, it framed a skull-like face. Dry, yellow parchment-like skin was laid over prominent cheek bones, decorated on one side by a skull tattoo.

Her desperately thin arms also carried an amateur-looking heart tattoo, though there was little enough room on those stick-like protrusions from which knobbly elbows stuck out. Her skinny hands resembled claws.

She wore only a "tank top" over her non-existent bust, her belly, flat and exposed, carried rings in the belly hole. Jeans hung from her hip bones - loose, torn at the knees, frayed everywhere. Her feet were thrust into surprisingly new-looking, name brand joggers (probably stolen).

An ancient battered and torn backpack dangled casually from one hand. In the other she carried a bag of lollies.

Beanie took her seat with extreme, considered care, yet seemingly casual - close to the door, able to view every seat on the train, able to flee at the first sign of trouble. Her eyes examined me. I feigned a tired semi-sleep, eyelids half closed. She'd seen me before. I had become a regular in my Muslim veil with cleaning props – just another ethnic office cleaner going home late at night. Those darting faded blue eyes slipped without haste over the other passengers, sizing them up – the drunks from the nightclubs, the couples, the pick-ups.

I'd chosen my seat earlier knowing her routine thoroughly by now. Better the chaser should be in front, never following suspiciously behind, enough to panic her. I'd put the cleaning bag on the inside seat next to me, like a very proper modest Muslim lady. If I had to move fast, I could dump the veil. It hid the gun.

I wasn't after Beanie. I was after the man she worked for. The cops couldn't find whoever was spreading some new, killer ice into the nightclubs. Six kids had died so far. Others were in hospital....probably mental for life. As a last desperate measure they had come to me. I'd stood in the shadows and watched and waited and followed.

I'd planned carefully, taken my time. Tonight was the night. I felt the unfamiliar gun pressing into my stomach beneath my loose clothes.

The train took off. Beanie's eyes gave a last nervous flick around the carriage, then she settled back, opened her bag of lollies and began to eat them. I recognised them as the kind I'd had as a kid – cheap, bright red pretend strawberries. She tossed them into her mouth one after the other, gorging them at fantastic rate, her arm moving mechanically from the bag to her mouth with regularity. It was the astonishing speed with which she downed them that struck me. These were not soft, pastel like lollies, but hard, chewy things. Why on earth eat them like that?

In my mind's eye I could see this street kid who had absolutely nothing, scurrying into a dark laneway with a small treat discovered, hiding away from those likely to steal it violently from her, gobbling it back quickly. The way she ate, the way she carefully folded the creased bag and tucked it into the rim of her beanie, told the whole story of her life. Loneliness, fear and depravation had always been her daily companions. Each movement of Beanie's emaciated arms showed all too clearly the druggies needle lines. She was dying.

How old was this street child? She could have been anything between fifteen and fifty. As I sat, my body swaying to the rhythm of the train, I was filled with a most incredible sadness for this creature...who had probably never been a child of anything but the streets.

City West, the last station before Perth, was closest to the nightclubs and the bad guys. Some tired looking bar staff trouped on. Just as the doors began to close, Beanie flickered off. Fast, but I was ready for her, standing on the platform half a carriage away, my gun drawn as the train wheels made an anguished metal tearing sound against the tracks and set off for Perth, taking what little light there was on a dark, cloudy night.

I held my breath and listened. There was a strange, metallic sound, hard to hear, just above a whisper. I moved in its direction, eyes adjusting to the light, seeing better as moonlight filtered through a break in the clouds.

I stumbled suddenly over what appeared to be a pile of rags. It was Beanie. I absolutely froze. The slight breeze carried the merest whisper of a curious metal sound behind me.

Spinning and diving, I fired blindly in its direction, loosing just one shot. There was a clatter as a metal baseball bat hit the ground, a thud as something heavier fell.

I snapped on my torch. A lucky shot had hit him right between the eyes.

Leaves began to blow past me. I realised they weren't leaves but dollars. The street kid's ancient backpack had spilled open, the contents of thousands of dollars blowing everywhere.

I turned back and looked properly at Beanie in the torchlight. Her shell-like skull had been smashed in completely. It was a body without a head. Blood, brains and human flesh were everywhere. I dropped my torch and began to howl like an animal.

She had been the dealer's daughter, his sex slave since a kid. He used her as a drug mule and to escape she had been skimming – that is why he was waiting at the station with a baseball bat – having done everything else to his own daughter…..

I woke disorientated by the bouncing of the ship, fell into a dreamless sleep. The last nights at sea, if I slept fitfully, I wasn't again visited by the old nightmare. I wondered whether it was really leaving me.

CHAPTER 6

Hong Kong

"Welcome to Hong Kong, Peggy." He was standing in the shadows near the dock gates.

"Charlie, what a nice surprise!" Boy, did I really mean that! I buried my face in his chest. He gave a wry smile and pushed back the upturned collar of my jacket, revealing the scar.

"I didn't think of Taylor for a while, dropped by the hospital on the off-chance. She practically jumped out of the bed on those broken legs to give me your message. Added you looked like you'd been shot.

"I put an all points on the local Immigration, missed you by a day. I might add that you may just lay claim to being the only person Lone Wolf missed. We checked the bullet – it was definitely from the same gun."

"I wanted to draw her out with my publicity...but that was a tad close and entirely my fault. I'd guessed the cell phone could be bugged somehow, then I picked it up and told you I was going down to **the station** to ring! How stupid was that!

"Now come and meet some old friends of mine."

I'd rung the Chans from the boat and a limo slid into view. Charlie shrugged and sat back for the ride as we powered to the luxury apartment area of Hong Kong, in the hills. The views were stunning but neither of us noticed as we held hands very tightly. Charlie was saying to me in his own way 'I nearly lost you' and I was saying 'hard to do'.

Chan was a banker - a very wealthy man married to Mi – five foot of mischief, now a publisher in her own right. Her recent sorties into the Chinese market almost made Chan's income look thin.

Mi burst out of the door as soon as we arrived and dragged me in. I hadn't seen her for a couple of years, but she hadn't changed – a ball of sheer energy, wrapped in a demur high necked Chinese dress, with long black hair that hung to her waist and green, green eyes. She seemed ageless.

I winced as she grabbed me and dragged me inside, still attached to Charlie.

"You're hurt! You didn't tell me…Lowell's here – isn't it wonderful!"

I'd put out an S.O.S. for my old friend Lowell, whose main assets are his undoubted wit and charm, boyish good looks with blue, blue eyes and a mop of blond curls. These serve to make him rise like champagne bubbles to the top of the social glass. He drifts around the world A-list scene with panache. Heck, I suppose *is* the scene by now.

Owner of a string of antique shops world wide, the dashing but savvy Lowell knew everyone in the art trade. If my hunch about paying the Lone Wolf off with art was right, he could prove invaluable in this investigation. However, even I would never have believed the solid break he was about to deliver.

Now everyone fussed over me and were nice to Charlie for my sake.

"It's ok. I've seen a doctor and had more than enough rest on the trip here. It just has to let itself get better."

We gathered around the table, the implacable Chan opposite Charlie – they were of a height and looked strangely alike.

"As you will have gathered, Lone Wolf took a pot shot at me, in Chicago, so I ran to San Francisco, taking this with me."

I produced the (now heavily bloodstained) file I'd purloined from the records office under my jumper the day I fled Chicago. It was passed around the table. The photo had a magical effect on Lowell, who turned it upside down, then read the file carefully.

"Well, the name is all wrong, Darls…but…"

"But?" we all chorused.

"In Italy she is known as the Contessa d'Alviro, happily married to Count d'Alviro for some years – his second wife. No children of their own. They live just outside Milan and lead a very luxurious lifestyle.

"I've stayed at Villa d'Alviro. Miriam's stepchildren adore her. They more or less run the Villa in their parents' absence…both parents are often away on business."

Now Lowell produced the absolute ace from the hat.

"Miriam is of course Dupont Galleries. The Count, a charming fellow, is rumoured to have dubious connections with the gentlemen of the south…."

"Mafia, you mean **The Mafia?**" Charlie croaked out, taking the file and scouring it.

"Yes."

"Now some things begin to make sense. We have previously thought of this killer literally as The Lone Wolf. If she has 'connections'…" His voice trailed away.

The possibilities were endless. Also, her abilities in the hands of organised crime were positively frightening.

Chan rubbed his hands with glee.

"Sounds like a really decent mystery, Peggy. You stay here now, see some of my doctors, get better."

"Seems like a good idea to me," Charlie kicked in. "Ball is back in my court, Peggy. I want you out of the firing range whilst I get into this new information.

"You've not only identified the Lone Wolf, but Lowell has broken the case open. We know where she lives. It's up to me now, with all my international connections."

I wanted to argue, but it was true. Charlie had the means to launch huge international undercover operations. He immediately rang and booked himself a seat on the next plane to New York.

Chan fussed around him, organising a limo to the airport. We walked down to it together, arm in arm.

"Stay safe, babe," he whispered, kissing me and then he was gone.

"Look like something serious, Peggy?" Mi emerged from the shadows as I stood staring after the departing tail lights.

"Early days, Mi. It was always going to be pretty much of a "fly in, fly out love affair" thanks to both our jobs. I think we both accept that."

"He very cute."

"Damn right!"

We laughingly rejoined the others. :

"You know, Lowell, your mentioning the Mafia was as good a way as any of getting the CIA off our backs, for all that I love Charlie. I have to say I am almost certain Miriam acted alone. The Lone Wolf murders are very different from mob hits – a single person acting alone. No, we have to took elsewhere."

To shake us from the seriousness of the high level meeting, we ate out that night and I indulged myself in the best Chinese food I had eaten forever. The next morning we split up – Mi to her publishing house and Lowell to an auction.

Chan complained less than usual about being shuffled off to head one of the biggest banks in Hong Kong, when I begged a lift with him into the centre of town to go in search of some of my "toys".

"Good. I wish to talk to you. Seriously, Peggy, your friend Charlie right in many ways about staying out of the firing line for a while. I want you to see some more doctors. You don't look too good. They will come to the apartment this afternoon?" He broached the subject tactfully.

I agreed. "That's fine, Chan. Thank you for everything. You may well be right."

On a less serious note I was able to add, "I hope Charlie hasn't put a tail on me – where I'm going they don't like policemen…they knife first and ask questions later."

Chan was thrilled at all this intrigue. He also knew I was right and that a Triad member could spot a cop a thousand miles away. I left him at the bank and took an underground train ride, then walked through the baffling series of alleys that are the very heart of the city. Nobody bothered me. I was a regular visitor to this district.

I'd come to Hong Kong just to meet Peter Yang. He specialised in acquiring the sort of "anti-security" electronic goods that are generally, to be honest, of more use to the bad guys than anyone. I wanted a scramble mobile phone, safe from electronic trackers.

"Very expensive," he muttered, "Very rare."

"Very urgent," I replied. We dickered over the price but my heart wasn't in it. Eventually I'd get Charlie's mob to pay expenses on this. Also, I expressed an interest in a few other electronic toys that had just come onto the market. Peter gave a wicked smile.

"I think you up to something, Peggy d'Sousa."

"Yeah!"

Mi and I met for lunch and went on to the Ladies Market and had fun buying me yet another wardrobe - clothes for the humid heat of Hong Kong. I was very, very tired by the time we got back to the Chan's. Too tired.

Chan's fancy doctors arrived and after a confab, took me to a nearby private clinic and checked me over again. Like the doctor in San Francisco, they decided I'd lost far too much blood and gave me some more, then tucked me in for a couple of nights. I slept most of the time, re-charging my batteries. I escaped with some more medicine and a feeling of well-being.

I had to admit I was feeling better than I had since the shooting by the time we gathered around the Chan's dinner table that night to discuss tactics.

"Where do you think Miriam is, Darls?" Lowell asked.

"I feel certain, Chicago."

I told them in detail about my visit to Chicago and Evangeline. "Lone Wolf strikes me as the same sort of person. She is a local who knows and trusts those streets. She's somewhere there."

"You don't think Evangeline or someone from the Police Records could have tipped her off?" Lowell asked.

"Someone certainly put her on to me. I would bet she still has some friends there, another life even. If she doesn't need the money in Milan, she might be using it for something in the US she wants to keep away from the good Count. She may not even know about his supposed contacts to the Mafia."

"Is not likely," observed Chan.

"No, that I grant you. The main thing is, thanks to Lowell, we know she's into art. How easy to pay her off with a decent picture that has a legal provenance. Yet this latest shooting is different from the others. It suggests something else…just a theory mind:

"We know Conseula and Henri shot through with some of Carpentier's drugs and set up their own game in Chicago. *Conseula* could have been the one to hire the Lone Wolf to shoot Henri."

"Taking over the business?" Mi was nodding.

"Exactly. Then Conseula paid Lone Wolf off with a bum picture…a very dangerous thing to do to the sharpest shooter in the universe."

"Conseula may not even have known it was a fake, if she stole this also from her father," Mi pointed out.

That was a very good thought. In fact it was brilliant.

So we now had a respectable motive and means for Conseula's death. But how to check it out?

"Leading art auction houses would remember if Miriam had approached them to check the provenance…" suggested Lowell.

"Any way to find out?"

"We-e-ll…*perhaps.*" That meant, 'of course, but don't ask questions'.

"So you intend to return to Chicago, Peggy?" Mi was shaking her head.

"That was the general idea."

Mi took a deep breath. "You remember what you tell me – after – after your last case." Mi had held my hand and got me through some terrible days after the Beanie shooting. She was the only one I'd spoken to in detail about the case, so distressed had I been (although I was certain she would have reported back to the others).

"What?"

"You quote Matsuo Basho at me:

'Old pond, a frog jump in, water sound.'

"You say a ripple in the water down in Fremantle had helped you find someone *no-one* else could find, because it is a pond you know so well, even if is a frog, but not the *right* frog, you will know."

"So?" I was belligerent, annoyed at being questioned.

"The Lone Wolf – Miriam – this is Chicago to her. When you turn up, she know something wrong. However, San Francisco – you can quote the streets chapter and verse. You have been there very often. Knowing you, when you visit, you don't go just to the tourist places, but to prowl the mean streets of today, am I right?"

"Mostly." These people knew me too well. Even when I went on business, or just for pleasure, I would racket around the "no go" zones. Streets and people talk to me.

"You have a feel for these streets, Peggy. You know people there. You will know who should not be there."

That made me laugh as I told them the story of the 'too empty' streets on the night of the cop car attack, of Lefty Four Eyes and his mates.

"Exactly! You realise people who should be there, are not."

"So if I get what you are saying, you mean, I shouldn't take Miriam on in her own pond, but somehow entice her to mine – and San Francisco is my home turf in the US?"

"It makes sense."

I could hear the others give a perceptible sigh of relief that I hadn't flown off the handle at the mention of my last job. I sensed a plot.

Chan now spoke, choosing his words with care. "Peggy, I think this Lone Wolf is very like you for many reasons. You said yourself you would have chosen such a gun. That is how you recognise it is a woman. She is in to very into hi-tech stuff, years ahead of her time… like you. You already understand her thought patterns.

"What Mi says has much sense. You have greater advantage in San Francisco, much street knowledge."

I didn't like to concede a point in my own investigation. I was itching to get back to Chicago, but everything they said made sense.

"You've all been talking this over for a long time," I accused.

"Yes."

"You seriously think I've latched onto her thought patterns?"

"Darls," Lowell chimed in, "That guy Charlie has been chasing the Lone Wolf forever. How long were you in Chicago before she was taking pot shots at you?"

"Well, sitting on that long, long boat ride, I'd worked out that it took more than my little TV publicity stunt to work. She had to know why I was there. She must have put it together with information that *someone* was feeding her, that I was going over to the Hall of Records for something…or someone…and she was likely that someone. No reason to take a pot shot at me otherwise.

"That's why my gut feeling still tells me to go to Chicago…" I said stubbornly.

"But…" they all protested at once.

"Where," I continued, "I will buy Evangeline the breakfast I promised her, stick my head in the Records Hall, then head straight the airport and hop a plane to San Francisco."

Mi spoke up. "My publishing firm has its Californian head office in Los Angeles, but it's time I visited there and suggested a San Francisco base and went looking. With all our new Chinese book titles we could make killing in San Francisco… hah- I do no mean that for real, you understand!" We all had to laugh. "I can set up a home there. It will be safe."

"That's brilliant! I will literally need a safe house there and soon."

"Understood. When you ready, ring Chan. He will have my new address."

The Chans had had a bad time with the Triads at one stage. They knew all about avoiding emails and mobiles.

Lowell spoke up. "We've had some dangerous assignments, Peggy, but this one…"

"This one is definitely 'Red Alert'."

Looking anxious, Lowell said: "You still have a key to my New York apartment? Run when you have to. I'll leave money in the safe there, just in case."

We all joined hands around the table. Despite my injuries, I felt better than I had in years. Something was *happening*.

CHAPTER 7

Fighting Back

Evangeline's eyes opened wide as she undid the latches on her door.

"You did say a Kim's Special Breakfast on any Friday?"

"I most certainly did! Come in, come in."

She fussed around heating up some coffee and producing plates, knives and forks whilst I made a space for the takeaway on a table between us. We both tucked in to a pile of hash browns, fried eggs and bacon and just about everything that was bad for human kind, not talking until we sat back to sip steaming hot coffee.

"Oh, I think I've died and gone to heaven," said Evangeline, kicking off her slippers.

"Sorry I was a bit late in delivery."

She put her coffee cup down. "I didn't know what to think. The 'boys' told me there'd been a shooting. Even my 'special underground' wasn't sure if you were alive or dead."

"Someone took a pot shot at me. I thought I'd better leave town for a few days 'til things cooled down. Here." I pulled a little package from my pocket. "The Chinese swear by this ointment for arthritis."

"Where did you get it?"

"Hong Kong." From Chan's top specialists. "Just rub a little on your hands once a week. Don't waste it."

She shook her head, then laughed. "My oh my, you private eyes really do lead an exciting life, don't you?"

"Too exciting sometimes. Oh, that coffee was nice. Let me…"

But Evangeline was insistent on taking the cups and plates and washing them up herself.

"Do tell me more!" she called out over the clatter of dishes.

"Not much to tell, really." I shrugged. "I knew someone was on to me, I just didn't realise they were that close." I showed her my scar. "I was at the station so I hopped a train to 'Frisco where I got stitched up, then grabbed a boat to Hong Kong to thaw out. Don't know how you stand this weather, truly I don't."

"Is the person who shot you still in Chicago?"

"I think so. Next time I'll be ready for them."

She looked at me. "I hope so, Peggy, I really hope so. You watch your back, mind!"

"Oh, I intend to. Unfinished business."

She pulled off her washing up rubber gloves and dried her hands carefully. "If I could do something with these…" she held her hands up in frustration, "I'd watch your back for you." A tear gathered at the corner of her eye.

"That's just it, you can. I need someone who really knows this area day by day. Something strikes you as just a bit odd, just a bit strange, let me know. It's local knowledge I need now. That 'special underground' you told me about is more vital than anything. Give me your phone number. I'll give you a buzz from time to time to find out if you sense anything."

"You are humoring an old lady."

"My last big case, no one could work out how I cracked it. It was sheer local knowledge…no, not even that, a feeling that something was slightly out of place. I'll tell you all about it someday."

We hugged and I left the little old lady, but only after I seen to it she *had* tried the ointment I'd brought her.

Time to head out into the cold of those Chicago streets, which was harder to endure after the heat of Hong Kong. The chase for Miriam began.

Dupont Gallery in Chicago turned out to be a surprise. I'd expected to find it in the old district, however, it was on the ground floor of a merchant bank, a modern glass skyscraper in the business district, tucked in blocks of similar soul-less buildings in new

Chicago, whose shadows made the drab winter day seem even darker, so little sun and light crept through to the pavement.

The gallery was shut and there was no sign of life.

Then I sought out the new shopping plaza where Conseula Carpentier aka Mrs Candy-Jane Dickerson had made her last struggle up the escalator. I wondered about her. Charlie had said she was well established in Chicago. I would have to check what he had come up with regarding her background.

I examined the crime scene, stood where the shooter had stood. I realised people glancing down casually may well have thought the Lone Wolf was just holding a mobile phone. It told me nothing else.

Conseula was running. Why? It's as if they'd had an argument, then she fled, being chased. The Lone Wolf would have known she'd be at the opening, may have demanded cash for the fake picture – or just said 'I'm coming to get you.' Something made her run like the devil himself was after her.

A wary guard saw me poking around.

"Can I help you, Ma'am?"

"Ladies jumpers? It's so darned cold out there today! This place is so big…" I shrugged my shoulders helplessly.

"Coldest winter I can remember! You'll find ladies wear on the tenth floor!"

I headed up the death-dealing escalator, again checking where that bullet could have come from. Opening day it might have been, but my guess was Lone Wolf had checked out the security cameras well.

I bought and put on some heavy jumpers, then stayed to have lunch at the upstairs restaurant, loath to leave the friendly heat.

There was no getting out of it, time to brave the great Chicago weather again. I walked down to the Records Hall and said "Hi!" to Harley at the front desk.

"Evangeline let us know you were back.."

"Can't stay away."

"She said youse was shot."

"Yeah."

He rubbed his bad leg. "Bugger of a thing."

"Aint that the truth."

We shook hands. I walked across the road to the old hotel. Something about this place gave me the creeps – more than just my unfriendly reception - so I was on my guard, but there was no trouble. They had kept my things in store. I picked these up and left.

I'd shown my face around town. The empty Dupont Gallery suggested Miriam was also lying low somewhere, but may have had her spies. There was nothing more I could do here.

The light snow was getting heavier. The airport was closed again. The roads were too icy for a hire car. Nothing for it but to brave the bad memories, head for the main train station and book myself an overnight sleeper to San Francisco.

It makes a difference when you aren't trying to stem blood or hurting – I relaxed and enjoyed the trip.

I took a cab to the Ramada again and booked in for a week. I doubted Mi would have been properly set up yet so didn't bother her.

San Francisco was "doing a Chicago" and if not actually snowing, it was freezing. I was glad of the three extra jumpers I was wearing under a new woollen coat, both warm and dark, which I'd bought in preference to a puffed up snow coat because it gave me more movement.

I was actually on a personal banking expedition to the tall towers of the CBD of San Francisco which are said to be the beating heart of the city today to check out that G&G's cheque had come through. It had, so there was plenty of money to play with. I pulled out a couple of thousand in cash. Paying off the likes of Harry had depleted my reserves, which I keep in a money belt. Some expenses you can't pay for by Visa.

Heading out on foot towards Union Square, I was absolutely floored to find myself walking past Dupont Galleries, San Francisco, also part of a large bank. I just kept walking up the hill. The same crest on the bank as Chicago. It spelled DAL. Of course, d'Alivera.

Lowell hadn't said, or didn't know, that the Count was in banking.

Back at the Ramada I rang Hong Kong. Mi had been working fast. Chan was able to come up with an address in the Mission district.

The night clerk from the Ramada had a grin from ear to ear.

"Not staying long, again, Ms d'Sousa?"

"You know how it is, Joe."

"Travel safe!"

"I'll try!"

I took a cab to the address Chan had given me. In the dark I couldn't see too much, but when my eyes adjusted to the gloom, I found myself standing in front of one of the famous "painted ladies", the glorious old homes for which San Francisco is famous – this one mostly white with gold trim. I had to laugh. I knocked and Mi exploded out of the front door, dragging me inside.

"Peggy! Just get off phone from Chan. He said to expect you."

She had flicked off the TV, divested me of my coat, pushed me into a comfortable chair and thrust a martini into my hand before I could speak.

"Any developments? Tell all!" She perched herself into a seat opposite me, with legs and feet tucked comfortably underneath her. I would kill to be able to sit like that.

"Not a word until you tell me, how on *earth* did you get this place?"

"A banker friend of Chan's has gone on holiday in Europe for three months. We have the complete run of the house and everything in it."

"I suppose that means we'd better leave it as we found it, without any bullet holes?"

"Is written in the contract," Mi said with a slow smile.

I looked around at the luxurious house. "There's no doubt this place is absolutely perfect. It's central, I'll be safe here...and I have a few new toys that might put me ahead of the game...wow, what a house. Inspection please!"

Mi delighted in giving me a tour of the interior, which was every bit as splendid as one would expect, given that, alas, the "painted ladies" are so well out of the price range of normal people, this was clearly the much loved home of a very wealthy executive.

I chose an upstairs bedroom that, fog permitting, would probably allow a view of the Bay from its many windows. At night, it was equally breathtaking, looking down on a whole sweep of lights of the city.

I sank onto the most comfortable bed I'd been lucky enough to discover since Hong Kong.

Lone Wolf's possible presence in San Francisco was a serious problem. The whole theory of being safer on my 'home turf' was blown…except I had a safe house and friends. It was also true I knew the streets better and appreciated the kinder weather. It was as close as I would come to Perth in the U.S. so it felt comfortable.

Tomorrow I would have to nail just exactly where Miriam lived. She could easily be living next door to us in the row of "painted ladies", or along with many famous writers and actors, be high on one of the hills accessed by steep zigzagging roads, so beloved of movies for car chases.

In fact, the more I thought of it, the more I felt that somewhere very high, with a total view of San Francisco, was the most likely. It was a problem. An area like that was absolutely security conscious. You could get shot ducking over a neighbour's fence.

I needed to set up some of my toys, but tonight at least I could relax in Mi's company. I would have to guard against bringing my dear friend to any harm. That was my last thought as I drifted off to sleep.

CHAPTER 8

Chinatown

Next morning, Mi got ready to leave first. She was visiting an estate agent with a view to leasing a bookshop in Chinatown. A limo drew up outside. The driver got out so that he could be identified.

"It's your Hong Kong driver!"

"Chan made me bring him. Part of the package deal. I also could only take this house because he knew the owners were security freakos. You only got to walk through the garden gate last night because I recognised you. Then I had to de-secure the door to let you in."

"Excellent. I fully approve." I knew the driver doubled as a bodyguard. "Where did he sleep last night?"

"He has bedroom above the garage, make sure car not tampered with. We arrange pick-up time."

Security had become Mi's middle name over the years. Lots of people would like to kidnap the wife of so wealthy a banker...and they had tried on many occasions.

She pulled a pert little coat over her usual slinky Chinese outfit and headed for the door, showing me how to activate and de-activate things. We organised to meet for lunch.

I watched her driven away, checked her car wasn't followed, then remembered my pledge to myself to keep her safe. Taking some of my toys, I went over the house with a fine toothcomb. Security freakos the owners were. Even the phone was scrambled.

Later, after closing up, I was drawn like a magnet to the banking area. The Merchant Bank DAL where the Dupont Gallery was housed was an enormous steel and glass edifice about fifty storeys high.

What was I missing? Of course, if both Chicago and San Francisco banks had a Dupont Gallery downstairs, it was odds on there was an enormous penthouse upstairs. All sorts of interesting listening devices could be on the roof, disguised amongst the usual bank satellite dishes.

I took Mi's advice and did some upmarket clothes shopping, hurrying to my lunch meeting with her. She threw open her arms, laughing, as she saw me.

"You look so chic I almost not recognise you! You have lost much weight also – this is very good. You should dress stylishly like this all the time, I soon find you a rich husband." We hugged and laughed.

"I like that lovely green silk top. It goes well with your dark hair."

"Now you're teasing me."

"No, on the contrary. Bright colours suit you. I've just realised how awful it must be for your to have to 'dress down' when on a job, whereas I am lucky enough to have to 'dress up' to impress clients." As we sat down I noticed the bodyguard had found himself a table also. Impressive.

"So, have you found anything?" Inner city San Francisco was notoriously hard to find a commercial spot. Mi pulled a face. "Try many agents. Only one come up with a property that sounds remotely interesting. He say it not far from Fortune Cookie factory so bring me much luck."

"So you're determined to go ahead with something right smack in the middle of Chinatown?"

She looked at me pityingly. "Books are in Cantonese and Mandarin. I should open a bookshop in Little Italy? If property no good, at least I'll get to buy some decent food for tonight, cook nice tea."

I didn't think Mi's food tastes would link with those of Evangeline, and be it said, myself. However, I couldn't argue with her marvellous cooking.

I told her I had some exciting new ideas on "our objective's" whereabouts, but being in a crowded restaurant, didn't want to go further than that. She understood. As we left, we were joined by our driver, who appeared out of nowhere and led us to the car. It wasn't wholly a bad life, I reflected, being a rich banker's wife.

We left the car on the edge of a park near Peter and Paul Church and worked out way by degrees towards the Cookie Factory through busy, bustling Chinatown streets. Occasionally someone would call out to me in Cantonese, or wave a greeting.

"You're obviously known here, and may I say your Chinese much improved," Mi grinned at me. But when it came to bartering for food, I left her to do the shopping and took over the direction map she carried.

The property was in a side street unknown to me. We wove our way down dismal alleys towards a rather ramshackle building. Outside was unprepossessing. It looked as though it had stood empty for a while. Mi said "That's the address? Bit off the beaten track." She stopped and looked around, trying to gauge from a seller's point of view what kind of passing trade this place would get.

"Hang on, let me go first." I peered inside. There was definitely something wrong here. I could smell danger.

"No," I said firmly, backing out. "No." I pushed her back onto the sidewalk and raised my left arm high in a pre-arranged signal. The bodyguard who had shadowed us was instantly there.

We were ready for the tattooed thug who came leaping out the doorway with a bloodcurdling yell. Triad. The bodyguard didn't hesitate. He stepped forward just a half step and plunged a knife deep into the man's heart.

Mi stepped back to back with her bodyguard. A twin of the first man appeared behind us, yelling. Before I could think, the diminutive Mi had executed one of those "Jacky Chan" circles, kicked him in the face and brought her stiffened hand down on the back of his neck. Behind him, another magically appeared and was dealt the same treatment. I was briefly aware that the bodyguard was dispatching a fourth triad member with his knife.

It all had taken less than ten seconds and I hadn't lifted a finger.

We looked around. No others, it seemed.

"Is usual, this Triad, to go in fours," said Mi.

The bodyguard wiped the blood off his vicious looking his knife. We headed back for the car.

"Wait!" I wouldn't let them get in until I'd been over it with a toy I carried. At least I could do something! It was clean.

Mi instantly checked in with Chan once we were safely home. Satisfied that his beloved Mi was safe, Chan was all for continuing the adventure, with the stricture that the bodyguard should stay with us that night, sleeping downstairs. I took the phone from Mi and asked a favour of Chan.

"Could you make very discreet enquiries about the merchant bank DAL? It could prove very important."

The good news was that Mi had managed to snatch up her shopping as we fled. Although a little scrunched, it was in good order. She was able to produce a brilliant meal that night, over which I told her my theories about the bank.

"Lone Wolf has been getting away with a lot of high tech monitoring. We have supposed all along this was just one person with something hand-held. Well, it might be, but if she is the wife of a banker, she could install almost anything on the roof of one of those skyscrapers. If, as I now suspect, she lives in the DAL penthouses, I need to see what she has.

"You know how I hate heights. You would be the perfect person to take a tourist flight in a chopper over the city. Take photos of everything, but concentrate on the roofs of the banks downtown." I knew a tourist chopper pilot we could trust. From now on, we couldn't take chances.

Mi was seriously excited to be part of the "game" (as I had expected). She also had much better cameras than I did. Best of all, it got her off the streets of Chinatown whilst I sorted some things there.

Next day, once Mi was safely away with a swag of cameras, I slipped back into Chinatown by the obvious method – skipping off a cable car and wending my way through to Jimmy Wong's discreet upstairs office.

His eyes opened wide as I walked in. Usually I was scruffily dressed.

"Ho, been some triad trouble across town," he said.

"That a fact."

"Lady dressed like you now was there."

"Really."

He chuckled. "Not to worry, Peggy. These were out of town boys elbowing their way in. Not popular. Come from Los Angeles."

"Figures."

"Aha. Most people, including local boys (he didn't call them triads) very glad they have gone to their ancestors. You wont get any further grief from the local community. Is there anything I can do for you?"

"Perhaps not. It's not your line, but a friend of mine wants to open a bookshop – all Chinese titles you understand – somewhere in the main drag. I'm looking for a likely spot that is safe and will make her lots of money. Something on a corner, perhaps. She will pay well and regularly to lease."

"She is Chinese, your friend?"

"Yes."

He sat back in his creaky old chair. "Los Angeles triads follow her, I think. Mrs Chan is very pretty lady, husband very rich."

"If the 'local boys' start to get ideas…" I didn't like the way this conversation was going.

"Wise to pay usual 'commission', keep local boys happy."

I shrugged. "She's from Hong Kong. She knows that. She also understands to the last cent what the going rate is, or there will be no deal. The final 'yes or no' is entirely up to her."

I gave him $500 out of the sheer goodness of my heart so he said he'd try and find time to look into it, although real estate wasn't his thing.

So the whole of Chinatown was buzzing and everyone knew about Mi Chan. That wasn't necessarily bad for business. Against which had to be weighed the dangers. If the local bad boys thought she had enough clout to keep intruders off their patch, they would be ecstatic, would look after her and her property themselves. If they thought she was going to be trouble, we had a problem. Mi understood these undercurrents as well as anyone. She could play it by ear.

Hearing sirens in the distance, in the general direction of the altercation of the night before, I discreetly exited Chinatown and treated myself to a very large steak for lunch at a restaurant off Union. I was unlikely to get too much meat at Mi's place.

I went home and rang Chicago from the scramble phone. "Evangeline. Anything to report?"

"Peggy, you're alive!"

"Some reason I shouldn't be?"

"There was a fire in the Records Hall last night. They found a body. Everyone assumed…"

"Well, the bad guys are out of luck, luv. Now calm down." I could hear her crying on the other end. "You say there was a body. Badly burned?"

"Yes."

"So could be man or woman?"

"Ye-e-es."

"You know, my money would be on that little bastard…sorry about the language, Ev, that works the night shift in the hotel across the road. Sort of guy that would take money to do a job and blow it."

I heard her sniff and blow her nose. "I know who you mean, Peggy. Nasty little fellow. Do anything for a buck. That's a good thought!" Then added bravely, "Just when I thought I wasn't going to be able to thank you for the good that medicine is doing my hands."

"Good one, Ev. You'll have to tell me about it over a Kim's breakfast one day. See you."

I hung up and instantly rang Charlie.

"Peggy, you're alive!"

"As a form of greeting this is getting *old*. Why should it be me? I am supposedly still in Hong Kong"

He laughed with relief. "I didn't think you'd stay too long. You forget Immigration reports to me. You took a direct flight to Chicago a few days ago. No record of you leaving."

"It snows in Chicago. That makes it cold and it also means your spies at the airport are home with their feet up."

"So why the call?"

"Just reporting in to let you know I am *not* the body in the records hall in Chicago. If it turns out to be a smallish male person, check over the road at that hotel you booked me into, see if they aren't missing a night clerk. Nasty little weasel.

"On top of which I've got a lot of questions to ask and some things to show you in San Francisco. Meet me in Union Square day after tomorrow. Oh, and Charlie."

"Yeah?"

"Love you." Then I hung up.

CHAPTER 9

Strange Facts

Lowell was putting in some serious buying for his 'American Antiques' collectors' sale coming up in the spring. It wasn't hard for him to dodge into some major auction houses and do some checking as he went.

He turned up in San Francisco and rang me for the address. When he arrived he was as amazed as I had been at the beautiful "painted lady" home. He explored it from top to bottom, being in the business, and didn't at all mind waiting until our hostess got home before swapping any information on the Lone Wolf. Instead he regaled me with stories of the A-list scene. Mi finally arrived, hands full of shopping, ready to cook an evening meal.

After tea we brought Lowell up to speed on San Franciscan happenings and I told the others about the Chicago murder. Then it was Lowell's turn. He had finally cracked the provenance mystery.

"Sotheby's New York. I went to them last. Fellow there remembered that the Contessa had asked to check the provenance on a picture not so very long ago, before bringing it to sale.

"He said: 'Funny thing, it was precisely the same picture a French lady had brought us earlier. If not that both were turned over to our Degas specialist – me – I wouldn't have made the connection.

"The French lady was most upset when she discovered it was merely a copy of something hanging in a private collection in India. However, the Contessa was more pragmatic…being in the art world.

She merely said 'I thought I remembered it was something like that, besides I spotted some things wrong with it.'

"We had quite a long chat over the flaws in the painting itself, which made me conclude it was definitely the same painting I'd seen earlier."

"The Contessa knows her Degas, apparently. The Sotheby's man accounts her quite an expert in the field."

"Did he tell the Contessa about the French lady?"

"He couldn't remember."

"But she isn't the sort of person one could fool easily with the pay off of a false Degas, apparently?"

"Most unlikely, Darls."

"Very curious."

Even as we were trying to work out what this must mean in the scheme of things, Chan rang.

DAL, he told us, was one of the best run, most admired merchant banks in the world. Its owner, the Count, ran around the world, dropping in suddenly on every branch, ensuring that all his workers "stayed honest", that is, did not make the same mistakes as some of the big banks whose distant agencies got away with all sorts of practices which had led to them losing millions, even billions of dollars. There was not, repeat not a breath of scandal attached to the source of the Count's wealth, which given he was from Italy…was something of a surprise.

There we had it. But what did it mean?

"So we now know that the Contessa has oodles of money, doesn't *need* to be paid for shooting someone and can spot a dud painting a mile away…maybe we were looking at it upside down."

"In what way, Darls?"

"The gun. Always the same gun. It was first used by someone who shot members of a gang he believed raped his sister."

"Ah," said Mi, "I see what you mean. Maybe these fellows who died were all part of gangs in the old days?"

"I looked at those Chicago records. They were frightening. An awful lot of policemen and women retired shot, or were killed. Evangeline says things settled down after the school shooting…but things may have happened *before* the school shooting. Things that were unforgivable?"

"Perhaps the Lone Wolf herself was raped by a gang?" suggested Lowell.

That statement had about it the awful ring of truth. But it was too pat. Most of all, it didn't explain the Chicago shooting of Conseula, the Paris shooting of Henri, or why someone had died in the attempt to set fire to the Chicago records.

"The answer must lie in the lifestyle of the Lone Wolf in Chicago. What I now need is to pour over those photos you've taken Mi and see if they can give me anything before I catch up with Charlie again.

"If anything, all our new information has simply turned a good guys vs. bad guys investigation into something a lot deeper. We just don't have enough information on any of the parties concerned.

"I just hope Charlie is on the square with us. I suspect he's the type who always likes to hold back some information on a 'need to know' basis."

I had to have a lot of questions ready for him when we met. Furthermore, I had to have some answers of my own. I retired to my room and my computer, to go over all the information Mi had managed to get.

Two days later, I could tell by the expression on Charlie's face he wasn't used to being ordered to appear at a certain place at a certain time.

"This better be good," he greeted me with.

"Did you discover who the body in the …"

"You were right of course. The night porter from the hotel across the road. Looks like he broke in to set fire to the records, propped open the fire door, then when the fire was good and burning…"

"Someone had closed the door on him?"

"Right. Then wedged it shut with a block of concrete behind. He died of smoke inhalation before the fire got to him. It's definitely murder."

"We need to go somewhere…let's take a cable car."

We clanked up a hill, through Chinatown to the end of the road.

"Glad we rode it to the end. I hear Chinatown can be injurious to one's health, these days," he said mildly.

"I am reliably informed that a Los Angeles Triad was trying to muscle in on the local guys. It's quite the talk of Chinatown. And no...I didn't lift a finger in anger against anyone." (Which was, strictly speaking, true. I hadn't had time!)

We found a seat by the Bay and I put it to him:

"So far, none of my investigations make sense. What is Conseula's background in Chicago that she should have become, as you put it, a well thought of citizen? Has she got a husband there? Why did she head for Chicago of all places?"

"Wondered when you'd get around to that. We've been digging. She lived in a flash house on nob hill and greased palms of politicians from city hall way up to congress.

"We think...only **think** mind you, that she was one of the "Mr. Bigs" in the local drug trade. By the time we unravel it all, a lot of high profile people will have taken early retirement in South America. Your turn."

"What I can tell you is this. Probably she paid the Lone Wolf to get rid of Henri with a Degas, furthermore **she already knew** it was a fake, probably swiped it from Daddy many years ago, but being careful, she'd checked the provenance at Sotheby's, but she still used it.

"The real riddle is that if Miriam is the Lone Wolf, she is something else - a Degas expert. One good look at the painting and she'd have known it wasn't the real thing. However, she took it and only recently had it checked out. Having had all her doubts confirmed, she then appears to have gone out and shot Conseula.

"What I need to know is, did she make contact with Conseula that day? That woman was running like the devil was after her. Surely she must have received a threat of some kind?"

"I agree with everything you've said. But if she was threatened, I don't know how."

"Oh, incidentally, I have it on good authority that DAL's chief, the Count, has absolutely no connection with the Mafia whatsoever."

"You lied to me!"

I held my hands up and laughed. "No. Lowell merely passed on gossip which he believed. The locals in Italy believe when a fellow disappears on business, he must be doing something with the 'gentlemen of the south'. The Count, however, is engaged in keeping a tight eye on his business – something for which he is famous in the banking world.

"My belief is, he's also rather naughty. To make sure his employees didn't gamble away half a billion dollars on the futures, he had special listening devices installed on the banks' roofs. Your people may care to examine the electronics in these photos. They can't be legal. The devices were obviously meant to keep a tight check on honesty, but obviously the listening devices can be abused."

"And you're telling me his wife can use them?"

"Does. So you will need this."

"What is it?"

"It's a scramble cell phone. All your guys should have one, but for the time being, just press 7 and you'll get me on my cell phone."

"There's no such thing."

"Compliments of the back streets of Hong Kong."

"Aha."

"Trust me."

He roared with laughter and walked away shaking his head then stopped and came back.

"Just one more question. When you were running, why didn't you head for my apartment and ring me?"

"Lead Lone Wolf to an apartment full of information about herself and a computer with a direct line into the CIA? Anyone seriously good with computers could have hacked into the Federal safety net in no seconds flat."

"Yeah, well…but we're safe out here in the open?"

"Safer."

He bent over and kissed me, then was gone.

CHAPTER 10

Confrontations

I was drawn like a magnet to the Dupont Galleries. They were open, so I walked in, hoping to glean some idea of the mindset of the owner from the sort of paintings on display.

I stopped with almost a knee-jerk reaction in front of one particular painting. It was really quite staggering. I just stood in front of it, my senses almost in turmoil.

"You like it?"

I jumped as the voice came out of the shadows.

"I think it's brilliant!"

"It's very second rank," responded the voice.

I looked at the agony and ecstasy that flung itself out at me from the painting, the blood and tears. Although it was modernist, its colours suggesting rather than being, occasional figures floated through it, like the spirits of the dead.

"Second rank? I suppose beauty is in the eyes of the beholder. To me it has the feel of the streets and the ghosts who permeate them. The lost. This painting seems to capture so much of that…" I fumbled for words.

"Angst?" suggested my companion, moving to stand alongside me, critically looking at the painting.

"I suppose that's the word I'm looking for. It's a little fancy, but it covers it. How much is the painting?"

"$60,000 and overpriced at that."

I turned to look at the salesperson, Miriam.

"You into a reverse sell or something?"

"No, I'm the painter. I can see the flaws. You're quite right, of course, about what I was trying to capture, but the brush work isn't up there."

"I don't know about brush work. Does it have to be? Some people just chuck the paint at their canvas and are called genius."

"I'm not 'some people.'"

"Do you still paint?"

"No. I gave it away. Just couldn't get…"

"Perfection?"

"I suppose so." Miriam was staring contemplatively at the picture.

"Does any artist?"

"Oh yes, the great ones."

"Are you overpricing that picture because you don't want to sell it? I won't take it from you if you care so very much about it, but I am prepared to buy it otherwise."

She chuckled. "I don't care **that** much."

I gave her my name, care of Lowell's antique store in Fremantle. I always sent anything there. He had a warehouse where he could store stuff until I got home.

"That's Lowell **Hanwright**?" she asked, surprised.

"Yes, an old friend. Do you know him?"

She looked me up and down, like they do in those posh boutiques, wondering whether you are real sale material. "You don't look like…"

"One of the A-list? No, Lowell and I go back a-ways. We tend to move in very different circles these days. In fact, I think at the moment Lowell is promenading down a red carpet somewhere with some top movie star in Cannes."

"Next week. As a matter of fact they are joining my husband and I on our boat for a party after the premier."

Lowell was obviously moving quickly. Good for him! I tried to keep my voice steady.

"The famous movie party scene. Fabulous to Lowell – boring as hell to me, I'm afraid."

I got another long, considered look. "I've never heard him

mention you…Mrs…er…" she looked at the shipping document I'd filled in, "d'Sousa."

"Oh, it's *Ms* Peggy d'Sousa."

"You collect antiques?"

"Old useless overpriced second hand junk?" Now I had to laugh out loud. "I guess we look at life from very different points of view. Never could understand how Lowell became a multi-millionaire trading in the stuff! You might say I am more of a here and now, 'people' sort of person. 'Things' don't loom large in my lifestyle."

"But you like paintings."

I went and stood in front the piece I had just bought. "I don't often buy. However, there's something about this one…"

We parted amicably enough. I was filled with a sense of frustration at having discovered little more about Miriam, whilst she had learned a lot more about me. Yet one thing was now certain. She would be away in Cannes next week. That could be very useful.

When I got home I found a note from Mi to the effect that she was looking at another property. She left the address so I hustled into Chinatown, where I found her haggling over property prices on a distinctly decent property on the corner of Stockton, not far from the Fortune Cookie factory as it turned out.

She waved madly as she saw me.

"What you think, Peggy?"

"I like it."

"So do I. Sorry I'm not being much help on the chase, but this is fun. Oh, and Lowell said to say goodbye - he say with luck he will be able to catch up with the Contessa there – but will definitely be sure to say 'hi!' to all the Aussie film stars he sees at Cannes for you."

We both laughed.

"Once the bookshop is fixed up, I will move in the manager from LA. She is from San Francisco, has a family here and is dying to come home. Will make a great manager of the new book shop. There is room upstairs to put an apartment. I hope you will then take care of the security?"

"You got it."

She hugged me. "I'm so excited by this new book venture. Thank you for bringing me here."

I walked through and had a good look at what would be needed, both for the shop and the upstairs apartment. I climbed out onto the roof and checked the safety.

It wasn't too flash, so I said I'd draw up some ideas and give them to her in the next couple of days. I could wait whilst Miriam set off to the Film Festival.

Back home, Mi reported in to Chan, then we went out for a celebration dinner down at Fisherman's Wharf, with the bodyguard ever present.

"I must go back to LA for a few days to get organised. Now tell me what is happening in the case."

I told her about my encounter with Miriam. Her eyes widened.

"*You walked right up and spoke to her?*"

"Well, it was a bit the other way around."

"This painting, did you know it was by her originally?"

"No. I just liked it."

"Fascinating."

"But she didn't – like it I mean. Remember, this is the lady who could pull a fake Degas to pieces at a look. She really does know her art, I believe."

"What did you think of her?"

"First impression was I liked her very much."

"That is very strange."

"Yes. I think so too. She made a good act at covering up knowing who I was and what I was. I am more puzzled than ever before."

I told Mi my plan was to go to Chicago whilst Miriam was in Cannes and take a look inside the private apartment of the Count and Contessa.

"I am betting the security system is the same as here in San Francisco for the bank and upstairs. DAL probably hired a security person like me to do all the US security in their banks. That means it will be the same. I took a good look around whilst I was picture gazing. I shouldn't have any trouble getting into the Chicago bank."

Three nights later, quietly entering the penthouse of the Chicago DAL offices I walked right into trouble.

He was older than Miriam, more beautiful even, in a guy sort of way. Tanned, slim, head shaved, absolutely buck naked, he was most dramatic. As was the blonde beauty he was cavorting with across the rug, she screeching with delight.

I was out of there so fast I almost met myself coming in. Question: follow her? Or…?

I stood downstairs in the shadows, watching and debating. About an hour later a convertible driven by the guy, with her still screeching with delight in the passenger seat, came tearing out of the car park.

That settled my private argument. With the coast clear, I gave myself a flat half an hour to get in, get a look around and get the heck out of there.

It took me five minutes to break in again. Then I went to work. I ran my torch over everything. The joint looked to me like a bachelor pad. I stole an interesting looking photograph, then skittled. All sorts of things were starting to fall into place.

Purely as a precaution, I waited half an hour outside the front, in the shadows. I was amazed to see the convertible burling back again, loaded up with cases.

"Won't be long Darling. I've just got to grab my passport and call a cab."

He off-loaded her and her baggage on the front steps and parked inside. So, they were headed to the airport – and where else would he be likely to take his love, than where all the action was? I slipped down the road to where I'd seen a main cab park outside a station, and headed for O'Hare. By the time the couple arrived, I'd booked and was sitting in business class.

They didn't see me as they charged on late, giggling, into first class. I knew it was them…I'd taken a small peek in the direction of the noise. From time to time I heard them as we crossed the Atlantic. It sounded like they were getting "juiced", to use a pleasant term, then all went quiet.

We all tumbled off the plane at Paris and headed for the Very Fast Trains. I went to book to Cannes, but the couple were at another window, booking to Genoa.

OK, so Italy here I come. As the train took off like some rocket into space, noise from the couple was silent as they slept off the grog.

I could see them a few seats in front of me.

I was, for the first time, able to pull out my bag and take a close look at the photo I had stolen from the DAL suite.

It was of two young Chicago cops in uniform – Miriam and with his arm around her, a sergeant. He was almost certainly Miriam's brother, so alike were they. Someone had done my work for me. When I pulled it from the frame, in neat handwriting on the back was: "To Mum, happy birthday, love Miriam and Alan."

So fact: Miriam has an older brother, name of Alan, who was once a sergeant at the same Chicago PD she joined. He now appears to live, possibly as some kind of security guard, in the DAL Chicago executive penthouse, where all those lovely listening devices are set up.

Just which one was the Lone Wolf?

Who moved in on Henri? Who helped Conseula set up as a drug queen in Chicago? Someone who could use the DAL listening devices for all sorts of hanky panky. Alan was stepping up as number one suspect.

Fact: Alan could have been the one involved in the recent Records Hall murder after trying to get rid of **his own** police record. It was a different MO, right out of character for Lone Wolf, but maybe not for Alan, who might be running things on the side.

Miriam had been washing the "pay offs" through Dupont Galleries. She just couldn't be written off as the Lone Wolf or his number one assistant just yet.

A heavy pair of knuckles brushed me. A fellow who was a movie caricature of the bad guy lumbered through the carriages, looking left and right. He wore a black bag similar to those used for computer "notebooks". On his bloated size it looked absurd. He must have thought so too, for he stopped near me and pulled it off over his head with a grunt of satisfaction, then headed for the seats containing Alan and Babe.

I buried my head in a magazine as he struggled back down the aisle and kept going. He no longer had the bag.

At Genoa, I took my time, watching through the window as the couple walked along the platform. Sure enough, Alan now sported a new computer bag. As "drops" go it was clumsy but effective.

It wasn't hard to follow the couple. Everyone was headed for the harbour, where the annual gathering of the fleet headed for Cannes was taking place. Problem, the harbour was crammed full of boats. I kept my eyes and ears open and soon picked up the blonde screecher and Alan. They were being rowed out in a bumboat to one of several massive private liners.

This one was called *Miriam.*

Al and his blonde babe struggled on board with hundreds of suitcases, requiring the full strength of the crew and amused attention of Miriam and the Count, who could clearly be seen and identified on the bridge.

After the fleet had sailed I took an overnight room at a pension, ate a delightful Italian meal in a tiny restaurant overlooking the harbour, then got a good night's sleep before taking the morning express to Cannes.

CHAPTER 11

Cannes

Lowell walked the red carpet and was much photographed himself, being twice as tall and twice as handsome as most of the Hollywood leading men around him. I wondered if he had then or at any other time been made movie offers, which he may just have laughed off.

He was variously described on the big screen TV's set up around the town as an English, French, or European billionaire – never a humble Australian millionaire, but he seemed to be having fun.

His beautiful and famous partner's gravity defying dress was worth squillions and drew much attention. The film being premiered – quite secondary in the scheme of things – was a murder mystery called *Suspense* and it too was receiving good wraps from all the pundits.

To my surprise, Alan and his partner had tickets to that same premier. They too could be seen walking the red carpet. This was, I suspected, the highlight of the blonde bombshell's life.

I knew that Lowell and his delightful movie star partner would be doing the party rounds so I found out where the "Aussie Party" was to be held. Getting in wasn't going to be that easy, until I saw Zac Turner emerging from a Limo. I'd worked as advisor on one of his movies.

"Peggy! Come on in! There's some folks I want you to meet." Zac had a new movie going, some heavies from Hollywood to back it and was calling for me to be advisor again. I met everyone. In the way of Hollywood, we did business, set dates and shook hands on a done deal. Zac started to carry on to the others about my heroics but fortunately was interrupted as Lowell showed up at the front door with his partner. She had already become the hottest item in Cannes, since the good word was she would walk away clutching an Oscar this year. Everyone from Hollywood surged in her direction, wanting to be seen or known to have talked to her, or already do business with her. Money men!

In the scrum, I found it easy to slide out of the shadows and offer Lowell a pink champagne.

"Darls, you do show up in the most unusual of places."

Lowell slipped the photo of the two Chicago cops into his pocket. He'd never heard mention of Alan to that moment, which made me suspect Miriam's brother was based out of Chicago and rarely went elsewhere. Lowell promised to follow up with the family. He and his partner left shortly afterwards.

I went hunting Alan. The most obvious place was down by the harbour, watching the *Miriam*. Eventually, Lowell and partner showed up for the party in their honour, Alan and Babe hot on his heels.

Both couples left, heading out to "do" the big name parties. Lowell and partner had invitations. Alan and Babe didn't have to wave a few dollars around either, as like me, they greeted some big name movie stars as they emerged from their limos, who recognised Al and were happy to take them inside.

Lowell reported by cell phone that some heavy trade was going on at these parties, big money was changing hands for something from a black bag Alan was carrying.

Lowell said it wasn't difficult to keep an eye out. Known users of drugs were despised by their peers and gathered together in a group. By the end of the evening Alan and Babe were travelling Cannes with members of that group from party to party in their Limos as honoured guests.

One simple fact emerged - Alan and the blonde babe had come to sell, knowing their market and did so for the next three highly successful financial evenings.

On the early morning of the fourth day Babe appeared alone from the *Miriam,* carrying the famous drugs bag, into which the money had been thrust as sales were made. On the principal of "follow the money" I tracked her to the station, where we boarded the express to Marseilles – a town I hadn't been back to in years.

At the station, an elderly man, silver haired and very well dressed, greeted her warmly. They chatted excitedly in French, before being driven off in a limo with minders all over the place. Babe went up in my estimation. Or down, depending on how you looked at it. Earlier that week I had passed her off as a dumb blonde – more fool me. She had been active in the drug sales, was carrying the money from them and what is more, it was an easy guess that French was her first language.

I rang Gerard Lefret, gendarme, more in hope than anything else. I doubted he'd still be part of the Marseilles police scene, it being so long since I'd met him. His cheerful voice came to me over the phone: "Nothing much happens in Marseilles, Peggy, especially promotions. I'm still here!"

I met him as he came off duty. He drove me to his a retirement dream – a little cottage on the coast which he was dying to show off to me.

"How much longer, Gerard?"

"A year, then I can walk away and live here every day instead of weekends. The cottage is a wreck, but I will have a lifetime to fix it up, when I am not fishing."

I showed him cell phone photos of Babe and the elderly man.

"Mitch Carpentier and his daughter."

"But I thought Conseula…?"

"A man can have more than one daughter. This is Cherie. You want to tell me what this is about?"

"No, not really. I want you to promise me faithfully that when we leave here you wont look up anything to do with Carpentier in files, or on the computer or mention the name, then retire in peace. Evil has eyes and ears everywhere."

Nor did we mention the subject again. We went fishing in an absurdly small tin boat, laughing and splashing each other. Like many useless fishermen we ended up buying a fish at the markets and cooking it back at the cottage, where we talked of old times and anything and everything but the good and bad guys.

He dropped me back in Marseilles a couple of days later on the way to work. He was now back in uniform and more official.

"I see you are carrying a new scar, Peggy. Be very careful of these people…"

'Zey aren't very nice,' I chorused with him. We both laughed. "Don't worry Gerard, I understand completely what you are saying." I touched the scar on my neck.

I took a train back to Cannes, which was still in party mode days after the last awards. It was easy to pick up following Alan around. With Babe out the way, he would leave the boat and make a bee line for the dingy back streets and the flourishing local drug scene – this time as a buyer.

One night he tried to hustle his way into the exclusive Club 5, without membership. He was deposited in the gutter screaming "Fucking Maggots! Fucking Pigs!" at those who had chucked him there.

Alan stood up swaying, in attack mode, aggressive, swearing and unmanageable as any druggie – quite a terrifying sight. However, the bouncer at Club 5 was nearly seven foot tall with plates of meat for fists. He biffed Alan in the stomach – I could hear the air going out from down the street and winced. Alan landed on the ground on his back. Then the club's more serious anti-trouble guys appeared, pulling guns.

Lowell suddenly raced out of the Club' main door. Of course, he was a member and always stayed here during the Festival. I was terrified in case he got caught in an affray that was turning decidedly nasty. Lowell tipped anyone he could see, grabbed Alan by the arm and dragged him into a cab, somehow getting him back to the *Miriam* in one piece.

I had to be patient and wait for Lowell to colourfully paint the scenario of what happened next as he'd stayed on board then joined the family around the table for a farewell breakfast. He laughingly mimicked the characters, so that I could imagine the scene.

Following some chitchat about the movies, Miriam broke in to say to Lowell:

"Thanks for seeing Alan home last night."

She'd obviously hoped Alan would thank me. So I told her:

"Chap gets invited in to parties all week, doesn't realise some places are private clubs, no-go zones to crash. Easy mistake to make." I tried to be comfortingly macho – all boys together.

Instead of adding his thanks or apologies to someone who probably saved his life from the armed bouncers, Alan just glared angrily at me. Miriam changed the subject in the uncomfortable silence that followed.

"I sold a very expensive painting from Dupont Gallery in San Francisco recently to a friend of yours … a Ms Peggy d'Sousa…sent it to your warehouse in Fremantle."

"Ah Peggy…she's a genuine Private Eye, you know."

Alan almost choked on the coffee he was snuffling. Then he put a silly grin on his face, made a gun with his thumb and forefinger and went "Pow!"

With considered calm (according to him), sipping his coffee as he spoke, Lowell added: "Trouble is, it's not all romance and Sherlock Holmes today. She was recently tracked down and shot at because the bad guys were using some kind of hi-tech listening device that could tune in to cell phones. Outrageous! Good job she knows how to duck. Homeland security have become very interested in *that*."

Lowell said he realised this last remark so clearly discomforted the whole family, he changed the subject.

"Trouble seems to follow Peggy around. I do believe she rescued a policewoman from a burning car in San Francisco not long ago."

"She was the one who shot the Enforcer?" Miriam was startled into speaking.

Lowell nodded. "Claims he had backup. Unfinished business to Peggy. That's why she's still hanging around San Francisco. Says the 'mean streets' talk to her. Gets more fun out of chasing crims down dark alleys than walking a red carpet."

"You don't?"

"Heaven forbid!"

"Such an interesting lady, yet you've never mentioned her."

Or she her brother Alan, Darls. So I covered by saying:

"Her choice. Often needs to keep a low profile."

Then Alan had began making a loud scene with one of the servers about breakfast. His plate full of food hit the wall. He kicked back his chair with a curse, threatening the server with a raised arm, then stomped up the companion way out of view.

Miriam picked up the chair, comforted the sobbing employee, then turned to her husband:

"I'm sorry. I'll get rid of him. He wont come here again." She stalked out after Alan.

"Now that," reflected the Count mildly, "will be one interesting conversation."

Lowell told me of this breakfast chat as soon as he hit the shore.

"Sorry Peggs. I probably gave away too much. I was very angry at Alan. If you could have seen the look on his face – it was as good as a confession that he was the one who shot you, and enjoyed it! Trouble is, the Count will probably just get rid of those listening devices and we won't be able to prove a thing."

"I don't think it will be that easy."

"Surely he just has to pick up a phone?"

"I gave Mi's photos to Charlie."

"So Homeland Security really are interested?"

"Depends. Even so, we have solid proof of what was on the roof of the DAL banks. My guess, probably only put there by the Count to listen in to staff, it took Alan to work out how else it could be used."

Reluctantly I agreed to catch up with Lowell at his Newport Spring Americana Auction. It was the least I could do after all he had done on this case.

CHAPTER 12

Chasing Alan

Both Mi and I had been away from San Francisco for more than a fortnight, arriving back on the same day at the "painted lady". We ate out. I, embellishing the excitement of the chase to Cannes.

"So what it amounts to, you aren't any longer sure who the Lone Wolf is?"

"Lowell is certain it was Alan who took a pot shot at me in Chicago, which makes him the number one candidate rather than Miriam.

"He also says no-one has even mentioned Alan before, which strongly suggests Alan could have been doing time tucked away somewhere and may only recently have come out. It means he'll have a record that Charlie can chase up. No prizes on guessing what for. We now know he does drugs, that he's in with the suppliers."

I pulled out my by-now-battered photo of the two young cops and showed it to Mi.

"He handsome, but she also very pretty. Make good movie star. No wonder the Count come along and marry her."

"Yes, they would have both made good movie stars, wouldn't they?" But how did that help the case? I gave up for the time being.

"Now tell me more about the bookshop." And the evening finished with Mi excitedly giving her plans for the new venture. It was no wonder her publishing and marketing ventures were such a success since she brought such enthusiasm to them.

It made me suspicious, however, when we got back home and

she was involved on the phone in a spirited Chinese conversation with Chan.

"What was that all about?"

She shrugged. "Oh, is nothing. Los Angeles Triads a little unhappy at what happen to their boys here. Firebomb our shop in LA."

"Nothing!! Why on earth didn't you say something? Was anyone hurt. What....?"

"Peggy. You stick to chasing Lone Wolf, leave Triads to me." She held my hands and looked at me.

"But..."

"I tell you something as a friend. You have recaptured – or begun to recapture – some of your old self, dashing off to Cannes like that. You enjoy the thrill of the chase. Emerging from a cocoon of sadness. Becoming butterfly again."

"But..."

She held up her hand. "Chan have enough troops on the ground to fight ten Triads. LA is sorted. No one is hurt. I tell Chan that San Francisco will be different. This much I know you understand. I am safer here than there, yes?"

"Ye-es, but..."

"So no more 'buts'. I give you the whole story once you have wound up the Lone Wolf caper!"

I opened my mouth to say 'but' again, decided against it.

"Have I really been wrapped in a cocoon?"

"You have been a worry. Not like you. You very outgoing. Now wake from long sleep, perhaps? It is not bad to grieve over a lost child, however little you knew her. Sometimes I think you grieve for all the children in the world. Carry too much. Let go, Peggy. Get on with chasing the bad guys."

We hugged. I was crying I know. Then I went upstairs. I knew what was at the back of my mind. Charlie had been unexpectedly quiet in all these days.

I pulled out my scramble mobile and dialled.

"Yo."

"Charlie, where the hell are you?"

"Watching the President eat dinner-and I'm bloody starving. Someone took a shot at him...as you would know..."

"I've been out of town. So, are you off our case?"

"No. I'll ring you."

I half didn't believe him, but I'd fallen out of the practice of scanning the daily press. I clicked on the computer and ran through the newspapers for the last couple of weeks. Headlines bristled with the attempted shooting of the President. If Charlie was the top man, made sense they'd call him in. The joys of being a trouble shooter!

I didn't get any further with the background of Alan and Miriam, so I left Mi a note on the table "good luck with the Triads" and ran off to catch the early plane to Chicago and Evangeline. Her eyes popped as I presented her with a "Kim's Special" breakfast. We scarcely spoke as we devoured it. Only then did I get down to business.

"Do you remember either of these cops?"

"Heck yes, that's Chic Delany."

"And *who* is Chic Delany?"

She then told me it was a popular TV cop show some years back . *Chicago* was the guy's name as well as the name of the show. Every cop she knew followed it because it was shot on the streets of Chicago; some of them even got walk-on parts.

"So this isn't a real cop, it's a character from a TV show?"

"That's right."

"What happened to him, do you know?"

"Went on to Hollywood, in lots of movies. He's even in the movie they say will take out the Oscar this year."

"*Suspense?*"

"I think that's what it's called."

No wonder Alan and Babe got to walk the red carpet!

"Do you have any tapes of the old TV shows?"

"Only the one my husband was in…and that is so damaged it won't play well any more."

"Suppose you let me take it away and get it fixed up, so that it will play like it used to?"

"Peggy, just to see *him* again…that would be wonderful!"

"Evangeline, I can't get over you. You help me catch the killer and end up thanking me. OK. I promise to take very good care of it."

She pulled a dusty tape from the shelf, into which she had inserted a picture of her husband.

"Looks like the wrong guy was starring in the show!"

"That's what we all said. Oh, it wasn't very true to life, but Chic was a handsome devil."

"You haven't seen him since – around Chicago I mean?"

"No. Too famous for us, I suppose. But, I don't know. Something seems a bit odd. I don't know what. Now I can understand what you meant about things not being quite right. If I can put my finger on it, I'll let you know."

"You'll qualify as a PI yet, Ev! What about the crew from the Records Hall. How are they managing since the fire?"

"They've all been given new jobs putting what's left of the old records onto computer…which means teaching all of them to use computers to start off with. Harvey was dead against it but needed the money. Now he realises he hasn't just learned a new skill, but can finally communicate with his grandkids in Boston, he's over the moon. If only these hands of mine…"

"Ev, you can just talk into some software and….never mind, I'll have to bring it along and show you or you wont believe me."

I slipped out into the cold Chicago morning and went back to my heated hire car (having learned the hard way about wandering around Chicago in the cold).

Sticking to my stricture of reading the daily newspapers, after missing out on the "presidential shooting" bit, I had come across a very interesting item of information. Chico and Babe were to attend the Chicago movie premier of *Suspense* that night.

A long session in the library now proved fruitful. Connie had bought her Chicago house from a family who made their money in the wild days of bootlegging. The article on Connie went on to re-tell the legend of the house. There were, it was said, secret entrances for escape from the cops, so that when they arrived on a raid the cellars full of bootleg hooch were empty.

I drove across town to an old fashioned Nob Hill, Chicago style. Big gates guarded massive grounds and mansions behind. I got lucky. A limo swept by me. All the secrecy in the world couldn't hide that the guardian who came out to the gate looked very familiar, being the big lug who'd brushed past me on the train down to Italy a few days before.

I cruised past, then all around. The place took up a whole block. It was heavily guarded. High walls were capped with the good old fashioned razor wire used on maximum security prisons. The place had the feel of a mobsters' headquarters. Why had Connie run from the safety of this to a crowded downtown shopping centre? Had little Cherie already moved in on her? I parked several blocks away and sighing, pulled my coat up against the wind. I needed to get closer. For once I didn't curse the Chicago climate. The grey mist and rain that had sprung up under threatening clouds were perfect cover. It might only have been late morning, but it was black as pitch. I climbed a nearby tree that had an overview of the grounds and settled in some cross branches.

Nothing to do but sit and wait and try and catch sight of the who came out of Cherie's house. That proved to be a no brainer in the dark weather, as dark saloons with heavily tinted windows swept out of the undercover garage.

I went back to my original purpose. How did one get in? By the time I was satisfied, the icy cold rain had been pelting down for some time, accompanied by great flashes of lightening and roars of thunder. I slid down the tree.

I tried singing in the rain as I squelched back towards my parked car. Windy City people called this spring? However, I was pleased with what I'd seen. Looked like the house was built in the old days, before electronics. The roll of razor wire around the top of the wall was imposing, but probably not as effective… and best of all, not updated.

The worry were the legendary "escape routes" which I hadn't found.

A hot bubble bath and a change to dry clothes in my expensive hotel room perked me up. Outside was dark and wet. Towards evening, the cream of Chicago society walked the red carpet to mingle with the new superstar of *Suspicion* starring good old Chicago boy made good, Chico and his beautiful blonde babe. I headed back to Nob Hill.

CHAPTER 13

Breakthrough!

I could see he was injured and trying to hide it. He waved me to the visitors' side of the desk.

"Lots to tell you, but – what the hell is it? Ribs?"

"Yeah," he gasped. "I was wearing a double 'vest' or I'd be fried chicken. Like they say, you should see the shooter – and his mates. They won't trouble us or the President again." He tried to laugh and a spasm of pain licked across his face.

"Don't laugh it off…" I longed to hold his hand.

"And you don't go soppy on me d'Sousa. Professionals, remember?"

He waved me back as I tried to get closer.

"OK mate, your call. Also as you said to me at our very first meeting, Charlie, first watch the tape."

Finally relieved of his Presidential duties, Charlie wanted an update and had sent a chopper to bring me to Langley. Why now became obvious. He should have been in a hospital bed. This guy certainly wasn't capable of walking around.

"As long as I sit in this damn chair, they let me come to work," he confirmed.

The gurus there had set about repairing Evangeline's tape as soon as I'd arrived and brought it to us.

"Probable change of ID of the Lone Wolf," I said over my shoulder as I loaded the tape.

The TV show was dated. It began with Alan, aka Chic, exploding across the screen, pulling his gun and to rousing music, shooting right at the camera '007' style.

I'd explained to Charlie that Alan was Miriam's brother, then almost jumped out of my chair, pointing at the screen.

"Hold it! Freeze the damn tape!" .

"What?"

"The gun," I whispered.

"What are you saying?"

"That gun he's waving around. It's **the** gun."

"Well, goddam!"

I'd caught Charlie's full interest by now. Still photos were run off of the tape's beginning and blown up. Sure enough, this was no stage gun look-alike, nor even the real thing that the Chicago PD carried, filled with blanks. This was the Lone Wolf's gun - or at any rate, the same type.

"You sure know how to capture a guy's attention, Peggy." Charlie flicked through the stills, laughing. Time to give him the rest.

"I chased Alan and his Babe from Chicago down to Cannes, to the launch of the movie *Suspense*. Took some photos along the way."

I showed him photo one, of the goon with the black bag on the train – and without it. Another of Alan getting off the train with the black bag.

Then a sequence of red carpet stills.

"Lowell with the leading lady."

"That guy gets around," grunted Charlie.

"Charlie and Babe. Apparently he has a role in the film. I thought Babe was likely some blonde bombshell he'd picked up who wanted to walk the red carpet. However, you see that Alan is carrying the famous black bag over his shoulder, full of expensive goodies."

I then produced some of Lowell's photos of 'goods for money' changing hands during the movie parties.

"Local police a little slack," he sneered.

"They wouldn't have dared raid a Cannes Film Week party. The whole country lives off such things. But you might want to take the names of a few of the US movie stars doing the buying."

"Probably we have their names already. Remember, we live off Hollywood just as much." Charlie spat the words out.

I told him how this had gone on for three nights, then how Babe had jumped ship with the money and taken off to Marseilles.

"She was met by a distinguished elderly gentleman at the station."

I produced the photo.

"Mitch? Mitch bloody **Carpentier?**" Charlie almost jumped out of his chair.

"Turns out she's his *youngest* daughter, Cherie."

"You're talking sister to Conseula, who bought it on the escalator in Chicago?"

I nodded.

Charlie allowed himself a whistle then shuffled through all the photos again.

I told him of the nudge Lowell had given the family about listening devices and of Alan's reaction on learning that I was a PI... that convinced him Alan had been the shooter in Chicago.

"Strange thing is, in all the years Lowell has known the family he's never heard Alan's name mentioned – famous as he undoubtedly is in Hollywood. It leads me to suppose he has a record, has done time. He's certainly in with the Marseilles boys. I'd say he's your number one suspect for shooting Conseula and for killing that desk clerk.

"Maybe we've got the real reasons for the fire skewered. Alan may have lied to Hollywood about *his* police background to get the part...perhaps used Miriam.

"*Miriam* was the real cop. Alan was the actor...yet I didn't guess it at first from this." I showed him the picture of Miriam and Alan together.

Charlie added the obvious. "Like you are obviously suggesting, he could have been real once, then got chucked out of the police for wrong doing, some background that made him want to burn down the Records Office. He obviously thought all along that you were after **him.**"

"How easy did we make it? He now lives in the Chicago penthouse of DAL. That gives him total access to the listening devices on the bank's roof. Could easily have overheard that conversation that I'd got the record I was looking for and was headed for the station.

"Babe, aka Cherie, now lives in the Nob Hill house bought by Conseula. This is the guy on the gate."

Charlie whistled again as I showed him the photo – and compared it to the bag drop off goon from the train.

He sat back in his chair: "Next, you'll be telling me you want us to raid this house."

"It's a famous old bootlegger's joint. The elderly reprobates sold it to Consuela legally. I can tell you, it's clean."

"You've been inside already?"

"Whilst some people were standing around watching other people eat…"

He managed a weak grin at that.

"I finally found the well documented famous cellars where the hooch was hidden in the old days. They are empty. The escape exits from these are bricked up. It is apparently local folklore that as the Elliott Ness types came in the front door, a quick phone call from the Mayor got the lorries loaded and driven out the back three tunnels."

"Uhu. And were the bootleggers ever charged or caught?"

"Nope."

"Then why **brick up** the tunnels, who did that?"

It was a very good point. Trust Charlie to put his finger on the same question I'd been asking myself all week.

"Straight, Charlie, I've just spent the last week going around the whole area and found no exits at all…I have no idea where the tunnels come – or came out.

"It helped that *Suspense* was premiering all over town and Alan and Cherie were red carpet guests for the better part of a week, a week during which I went through the inside of the house with a fine toothcomb on more than one occasion and had found nothing of value. I had expected tons of drugs, a cache of arms, something – or better yet – the names of people connected to either Conseula or Cherie. All I found were empty cellars.

"PI's might be two steps ahead of the police, but someone is two steps ahead of me and I don't like it. It scares the absolute shit out of me."

I hesitated. "All that I can think of, I did make contact with just one person, a friendly gendarme in Marseilles. He was about to retire, had the 'shack' of his dreams to retire to. I hate to cast aspersions on good old friends, but I cant think how else…"

I left it all unsaid. Bribery, torture, murder – however. I didn't really want to know and gave his name to Charlie to find out.

"That means they probably know all about you," mused Charlie. "So why are you still alive and walking the streets?"

"All I can think of that makes sense is that Alan has become one big liability to them. Heck, we aren't after the Marseilles mob – they know that. We're after Alan."

"Why not just take him out themselves?"

"Then we'd have to chase *them* for his murder. No, far more clever to have us catch him and put him away. They've cleaned up after Conseula. She might never have existed. I do wonder what Miriam's role in all this is. She seems to have some power over Alan…"

"If he's a druggie that counts for zero. She's in danger too. We need to pin him for Conseula's murder."

"We need the gun – and **backgrounds** Charlie. Get me backgrounds on all this… and for crissakes stay in that damn chair!"

I walked to the door, changed my mind and walked straight back to him, landing a passionate kiss that could have been seen by the whole CIA.

"Foxy lady," grinned Charlie.

I flew back to Chicago feeling good. Instead I walked into a nightmare.

CHAPTER 14

Dirty Pool

I called in at Ev's with her precious tape, feeling good. I found her lying like a bundle of old rags, half in, half out her doorway. She was battered, bruised and very cold…but emitting sad little mewing sounds like a hurt kitten, which meant she was still breathing.

In a panic I called everyone I could, starting with emergency and ending with Charlie. I rushed inside and got a blanket to tuck around her.

It was clear her little home had been tossed.

I travelled with Ev to the hospital where I was joined in my pacing by Harley and some other guys, once word got out – probably through one of the cops on the beat.

I gave a statement there to a beat cop, telling him how the apartment had been trashed. I couldn't believe the cautious Ev would have opened her door except to someone she knew.

Hours later, I sat at the bedside by her fragile body, her wrinkled face puffed from red and black bruises, eyes bloodshot. It was a body from which life was clearly flowing every minute. Although she had a lot of bruises she had surprisingly few broken bones. However, she hadn't just been beaten, she'd been **raped** as well. When I heard that, I don't think, ever in my life, I had been so angry. It was a hard, cold anger.

Seconds dragged past. Ev's pulse slowed. Doctors and nurses came in, looking more and more serious. I finally had a last desperate idea and got a tape video recorder moved in. I put in the tape I'd brought back from Langley explaining that I hoped some view of her husband might revitalise her. Obviously, the medicos believed there was nothing to lose at that point.

She flickered back to life at the sound of the tape starting and picked up.

"Brian," she clearly whispered as a hulking cop stalked in to one scene. We froze the tape so she could see it. She nodded and settled back on her pillows with a smile.

I hung on to one of her hands and whispered: "Fight, Evie, fight. Brian would want you to."

Nothing much changed for hours. I was only vaguely aware of people coming and going – doctors, visitors, cops. Evangeline was clearly in a life and death battle and I didn't dare move, sustained by my own anger.

Her eyes flickered open.

"Peggy," she whispered. "It was Chico."

"Did this to you?"

She nodded and settled back with a smile. For a minute I thought we were losing her, but then I realised she was smiling at Brian's picture.

Two doctors came in to do a re-examination.

I disentangled my hand and stood back.

"Pulse is stronger. She's sleeping now. It will do her good," one said to the other.

A cop sauntered in. Turned off the video.

"I'll need this as evidence," he said.

That jarred. Evidence? Evidence for what? I looked more closely, and saw Alan aka Chico in policeman's uniform, headed out the door with the tape.

"Stop him!" I yelled. "Stop that cop! He's the one beat up and raped Evie!"

But he was out the door and out the main hospital door before anyone could grasp that the person in uniform dashing past shouldn't be there.

When I told them what Ev had told me, everyone took off after Alan. I stopped to get on the phone to Charlie.

"Ev said it was Chico. He was after the tape – that's why he broke into the apartment. Now he's got it. Just walked in here and took it!"

"Beauty, gives my people a chance to get a Judge's signature to search that penthouse, find that gun." He clicked off.

I was glad someone was happy about something. I was seriously unhappy. Alan was now on the most wanted list in Chicago. Where did that leave the vulnerable Evangeline, the one woman who could put him away for something, anything? In great danger.

I sauntered in to her room, scooped the tiny, fragile woman up into a wheelchair, bundled blankets around her and took off down to the main entrance. If Alan could do it, so could we.

No one even thought to query us as I wheeled Ev out into the car park, tucked her neatly into the little bed in the small van I'd bought to use for surveillance on the mobster house in Nob Hill, filled with all my "toys" and them some.

I pulled in to a truck stop, pulled out my scramble cell phone and for extra good luck, spoke in Cantonese. If there was a person more can do on the planet than Charlie, it was Mi.

Evangeline was loving every second. When I broke out into Chinese she actually laughed.

"We aren't going to Hong Kong are we?" she asked.

I climbed in next to her. "Not quite, but somewhere safe. You are about to become very hot property."

"Why did Chico want that tape of my Brian?"

"It was the beginning, Ev, where he comes out shooting his gun…you know the bit? The gun on that tape is the same one used in that high school massacre so many years ago. Chico got hold of it – possibly initially only because it was light and easy to play with. But he shot a lot of people with it too.

"We think Chico was responsible for the Records Hall fire and the death of the young man inside. He's covering up the past.

"Question is, how did he know you had that tape?"

"That's easy. Brian said they could use our apartment as a set when they were making the episode he's in. I met all of the TV people – fed them coffee and sandwiches over about a week or so. Chico gave me the tape, autographed by him as thanks. I'm sorry, I didn't realise he was one of the bad guys. I'd have never have opened the door to him…"

"Probably he heard from someone in Records that you were helping me out. You took this beating because of *me* Ev, not because you were careless. He was afraid you'd show me that tape and I'd recognise him and the gun…and I did.

"Now the net is closing on Chico, you are going to be the most important witness in history. "

"Wow! I dig that!"

And she did. The long drive, taken easily with lots of with pull ins, was doing her no harm at all.

She was snoozing as I pulled to a halt three days later.

"Something wrong?" her voice quavered.

"No. We are there."

CHAPTER 15

Undercover

I was watching by camera from the next room as Evangeline woke up slowly, trying to take in her new surroundings. Her face was easy to read. She rubbed her ears. Obviously she could hear sounds of traffic and the murmur of voices from the busy street below her window, which made her smile. I had known all along that a city girl like her would have died if stuck somewhere deep in the countryside.

She got up and hobbled over to the window, peeking through the curtains, standing back so as not to show herself. Good, she was careful. But I would have to warn her about staying out of sight.. She smiled at the sound of the clanging of a cable car bell. Obviously she realised instantly she'd been stashed away in San Francisco.

"Well, goddam!" she muttered.

We'd moved in a large bed, set so that she could lay and look out at the sky and the rooves. The room was heated, for her hands. As for the rest of her, we just had to hope she would mend physically and knew that mentally it would be harder.

She went inside her private bathroom, closing the door. One had the feeling that the privacy was much appreciated. Coming out, carefully closing the door, she turned and saw me leaning against the opposite door, grinning, watching her.

"Like it?"

"Yep."

"Would you like to put on some clothes then come and look at your other rooms?"

The look on Evangeline's face suggested she would love to get out of her baggy nightgown.

"You're still a bit stiff and sick, so Lisa here, who is a trained nurse-cum-massage expert, will help you bath, just for a few days and replace your dressings, no help for it, I'm afraid. Nothing worse than someone invading one's very personal privacy."

Evangeline gave in with good grace, although her face said it all. Lisa was special and within a few moments sounds of splashing and laughter could be heard from the bathroom as Evie was treated to a bubble bath and hair wash. With her wounds gently dressed, she re-emerged in a Chinese style dressing gown, to make a selection of her clothes for the day.

Bringing up the rear, with all the old bandages, Lisa tossed me a nod and a smile. Our patient was on the improve.

"Oh my!" Evie gasped, opening the wardrobe door, clearly at a loss to make a choice.

"Perhaps something warm but loose?"

"Mi is your landlady and the best dresser on three continents. I'll make proper intros once you are dressed – but take her advice."

We retreated and left Lisa to help Evie dress and do her hair. "Bee-yoo-tiful!" she said, adding the final touches in front of the mirror. "Now you go join Peggy and Mi – if they recognise you, that is!"

We stood up, applauded and whistled as she came in, showing off her choice of a bright, aqua-coloured kaftan, covered in dolphins and sea lions. It was dramatic and cheerful, yet loose enough not to rub her wounds.

"I've died and gone to heaven!" she said happily, snuggling into the big chair and gazing around her. "Now where am I? San Francisco I gather…"

"Chinatown. In short, in the apartment above my bookshop," replied Mi.

Then I rowed in: "Now, let me explain something about Mi, aside from her being a nice person, my very best friend and all that. She's married to a rich Hong Kong banker. That means they have had bad triad trouble over the years. Mi has forgotten more about security than you will ever remember. Her husband, Chan, insists on her travelling with a personal bodyguard. Mi isn't bad at the kung fu type of stuff herself…just a few weeks ago they knocked off four bad guys not far from here.

"Knocked off? You mean…"

"Yes, Evie. You don't muck around with these guys. Chan is delighted he can beef up the anti-triad troops around his wife, so when we put out a call for specialist…er…"

"Muscle?" she suggested.

"Quite…he was only too happy to oblige. Now if there is a rumble, press this. Your own personal guy will come straight to your side." I hung an alarm buzzer around Eve's neck. "Press it now, to see what happens."

A huge Chinaman came slamming through the door and stood next to Evie.

"Evie, this is Ho," said Mi. "So that you can recognise him in a hurry, he'll be the guy with the red stripe on a black uniform."

Evie looked up into Ho's battered and scarred face. "Thank you Mr Ho." He bowed, winked at her and left.

"My goodness, he looks like a one man army."

"Before anyone gets to Ho, they have to get through our outer defences, which we have placed at various doors leading up to this apartment - about ten well trained experts, all fully armed, as well as all sorts of security alarms, cameras and so on."

"Gracious!"

"That's the good news, Evie. The bad news is that Chico is still on the loose. Once he grabbed your tape he made a run for it. There is every possibility that he also headed for San Francisco. That means you are in very big danger. If you poke your nose outside just at the moment, word could get back to him where you are. Remember, don't even show yourself at the window."

"Understood," she said weakly.

We all moved slowly and carefully to the little kitchenette. "The doctors have laid down a minimum diet – they'll be popping in from time to time to see how you are going. It's definitely time you ate and drank something today. Just for the time being someone will cook your meals…but after a few days you can do your own thing if you want to…"

"My hands feel better," she declared out of nowhere.

"Those Chinese doctors again, Evie. They've been putting stuff on your hands."

Mi stood at the sink, tossing things together.

"I'm not going to have to eat cat, am I?" she whispered to me.

Mi turned with a look of fake annoyance, hands on hips, then laughed out loud. "Numero uno, I vegetarian, so no cat, dog or anything else. Next, any food I cook healthier than anything *Peggy* likely to give you."

"Like 'Kim's specials'," I threw in.

"Whatever *they* are, I bet they have too much fat, not right things.

I winked at Evie. "Mi and I never agree on correct diet, but since you are still not well, we'd better stick to Mi's recipes."

The three of us sat down to a lovely breakfast and hot coffee.

"The doctors say you can get up for a little while, maybe stay up and watch some telly, but probably a good idea to take an afternoon nap."

We helped Evie back into her big chair, which she had already made her own, clicked the telly on low then tiptoed out as she was already fast asleep.

"Like to see you separate her from that chair again!" I said to Mi as we went downstairs.

Mi was going to run her shop for the next couple of weeks (or however long it took). I waved goodbye and set off. There was someone I had to see.

CHAPTER 16

High Noon

"Come to buy, Ms d'Sousa?" The voice swam out at me from the dark. Darn, I'd have to practice that technique.

"No. Pretty as those these pictures are, I've come to leave a message for your brother Chico…"

Miriam shook her head.

"You remember Chico, your brother, the guy whose convertible is parked downstairs.

"First up, he better hope and pray that the cops find him before I do, after he beat up and raped an old lady I happen to call my friend."

She blinked. "That's not even half funny."

"*Half funny!* If you could have seen that sweet little old lady when he had finished with her, *darling,* that is the understatement of the century!

"One thing I can tell you. Half of Chicago would love to tear Chico limb from limb. He knew that. Which made it a pretty sure bet he'd head straight for San Francisco.

"Next up, tell him his sweet little Cherie and the Marseilles mob have sold him out. He'll do better to turn himself in to the police."

"Very colorful," she muttered, frowning.

"It's over, Miriam. I don't know what part you have played in all this, but it's o…."

There was an almighty crash. Chico appeared, gun in either

hand. One of the 'pictures' was a see-through mirror and door, which explained Miriam's ability to suddenly appear out of nowhere.

"Over, darlin'? Not 'til we sort something out."

He dropped one of the guns on the floor and kicked it in my direction. "You're supposed to be so good with a gun. Let's do it!"

"Oh, you mean 'High Noon' and all that jazz? Two gunfighters in the main street?" I spoke sarcastically, prodding at the gun with my toe, then looked more closely at Chico's gun. Neither was *the* gun, or I might even have been tempted. "Don't like guns, myself. Never have." I kicked the gun on the floor away slightly.

That Chico intended to kill me I had no doubt. Time to talk, Peggy, keep his mind occupied.

"I don't get it, Chico. I can understand you breaking into Evie's flat, but why *rape* a 70 year old woman? I've seen you canoodling with the young and pretty – you're able to *get it.* I just don't understand." I slid my hands into my jacket pocket and waved my coat open, shrugging my shoulders.

"It makes no sense." In all this arm waving, I'd managed to get my own mini-gun nicely out of its arm holster. It slid down and nestled in the palm of the hand that was thrust deep inside my pocket. I softly clicked off the safety.

"Years ago her old man and I were on the force together. When I became an actor – despite the fact that I'd given him a part in one of my shows – he called me a fairy for leaving the cops. *Me – a fairy!*" He spat. "I told him if he ever called me that again, I'd do his old lady. He did. I wuz just carrying out my promise."

"God man, how many years ago was that? Evie's husband has been dead for years. She's an old lady. There's something seriously wrong in the head with young blokes who do over old ladies."

"You told me they were making all that up…" Miriam turned on him, shocked.

"I'm a man of my word." He thumped his chest. "Chico tells you he's gunna do something, he does it, better be sure of that. Now you - go for that gun. Let's see which of us is the best shooter in the world."

"Oh, I am," I said and pulled the trigger of the gun in my pocket. Chico grabbed at his family jewels - his balls - his manhood, whatever you want to call them - and screaming, hit the floor. Despite his pain, he managed to roll over and started shooting wildly in my direction. Something resembling a Jackson Pollock original went crashing to the floor behind me.

I heard Miriam whimper, but if for her brother's pain, or the devastation wrecked on the fine art I shall never know.

I was out of there fast, running as if the hounds of hell were after me. I slipped through cracks in buildings and headed for the Bay, where I took a ferry, dropping my little pea-shooter gun into the water about half way across.

My special phone rang.

"Evie has been calling for you." There was an anxious note to Mi's voice.

I didn't go direct to Chinatown. I couldn't after where I had just been in case I was followed.

"Where have you *been*?" Mi hissed when I finally got to the bookshop.

"Shaking any possible tails. Is Evie OK?" I ran upstairs. Evie was back in bed, looking distressed.

"Peggy, Peggy, I thought you'd never come. You see, I finally remembered."

"Remembered what?"

"I told you once before when I rang from Chicago that something seemed out of place, but I couldn't put my finger on it."

"And...?"

She dropped her voice conspiratorially and whispered to me.

"Are you sure?"

"Absolutely!"

We chatted for a little while longer. Evie had made a supreme effort to stay awake for me. She closed her eyes and was instantly asleep. I kissed her and strolled into the living room.

"OK, you going nowhere until you tell me what that was all about?" Mi was furious.

"That, my dear Mi, was all about 'Old ponds and a frog jump in, water sound.'"

"Spare me the literary quotes, just give me the facts."

"A few weeks back Evie sensed there was something wrong. She's pretty sure what it was now. I have to go to Chicago to check it out. I'll hole up in her apartment." I held up the keys she had just given me.

"Whilst I'm there I can bring any of her papers and personal things."

"You think the place will not be watched?"

"In case Evie turns up? Both good guys and bad guys might come knocking on the door. Sorting the 'who wants to know' into either camp could prove a problem. There are many more rats operating around Evie and that old Records Hall that we haven't figured yet. I'll drive my old van so I can take more firearms for protection as well as some mini cams and recorders."

Mi had not missed that, in all this chatter she was still to learn Evie's great secret. To divert her I told her I didn't think Chico was about to come running, and why…and his story about the rape.

"You can tell Evie whole the story when she wakes up."

"You just leave them? Not call cops?"

"What could I have pinned on him? He didn't have the Lone Wolf gun. He would have denied everything. Marion would have backed him up. She has the money and he has the fame to have me thrown out of the US or tossed away in a dim, dark cell.

"This way, he pays – sorta – for what he did to Evie. But we are going to need a lot more evidence. I'm still not sure about Marion. One of them must make a move. Seriously. Stay on you guard big time. I'll report to you and you report to me every day on a regular basis."

CHAPTER 17

'Old Pond'

I stared from the window of Evangeline's flat. For once the weather had improved. The two coppers on their beat didn't wear raincoats, just their normal uniform. I photographed them.

Evie was quick. She had noticed two things. First up, cops had stopped walking the beat in this area twenty years before. Second up, their uniform was all wrong. It took an ex-cop's wife to notice stuff like that. These guys carried guns, nightsticks and radios.

They paused, looked up and down the empty street and one of them spoke into the radio clipped to their tunic lapel, then continued on their way.

A lorry lurched out of an old warehouse at the top of the block, past the cops, then on its way. It had taken me two days to figure. Always the same pattern. These were just lookouts – very clever lookouts. Night time I would go look at the warehouse. Meanwhile I passed the time by going to the movies. I watched *Suspicion*, in which Chico played a good cop. A good cop, I realised, who wore a San Francisco uniform.

I dialed Taylor.

"When they filmed the movie *Suspicion*, was it filmed in and around San Francisco?"

"Sure was. We took that Chico guy around, showed him the ropes."

"He ever on the night patrol?"

"Yair. Me 'n Chuckie…"

"Same route you were ambushed?"

"Ye…ah."

I rang Charlie at once. "You holding out on me, Charlie?"

"As in?"

"Chico, was he a cellmate of the Enforcer? If so, what movies did he make in towns, playing a cop, where a cop was killed? And did you know all about this?"

"Yes, don't know – and no."

"You do realise Chico could have been the prime planner in all those cop killings?

"Where's Evangeline?"

"Safe – damn sight safer than Taylor in San Francisco. Get some protection on her…I can't do every bloody thing!"

"Where the hell are you?"

"Chasing bad guys."

"That sounded like the rattle of an El going past."

"So, Mr. Big Ears?"

"Watch yourself, Chicago is a tough town Peggy."

I fully intended to.

That night I went out at midnight in decent cat burglar gear and with house breaking toys. The warehouses down the road might have looked old, but they didn't have nice big padlocks on the big doors, or rattling, ancient doors that were dragged open to let trucks out. On the contrary, they opened smoothly, on runners, from an inside electronic switch.

I had cased the joint from before. Blowed if I could find an entrance of any other sort. That left the roof.

Behind the tangle of buildings next to it, an old alley-way with a fire escape going clear up to the roof offered the most hope. Just my luck. I was only half kidding when I'd talked Mi into doing the fly-over of San Francisco. Two steps off the ground is about my limit.

On the other hand, I have shed some weight over the years. I'd had no trouble at all setting up the safety stuff in the Bookshop roof in Chinatown. I told myself this over and over, as I climbed the fire escape to the third floor and jumped with a great prayer to the private eye's maker.

I landed softly and looked around. No-one on the roof, but

plenty of electronics. Here was the rub. They couldn't see the street – hence the fake cops. But *who?*

I let myself down to the deserted office level, above an empty warehouse. There wasn't a file cabinet, desk or sheet of paper in sight in the offices.

Then I heard rumblings. Squeezed into a dark corner, I watched fascinated as the old mechanics' bay opened. Two trucks emerged from the deep and drove out, parking near the door. It reminded me of trucks being unloaded from a vast car container ship. The drivers slipped noiselessly away down their hole. This operation was run from somewhere else. This? More like *these.*

I was guessing **three.**

Once the drivers had gone, I used my toys to make sure I wasn't setting off any alarms, checking the trucks. They bore the brand name of a flour company and inside were stacked several packets of flour…much as I'd remembered seeing them go out from a flour mill just down the road from me at home.

The difference, of course, was that the white powder in these packets wasn't flour, but white death – heroin, trucked in maybe from the Lakes, enough to feed a whole country.

I went out the way I'd come in. If I'd missed a camera, I had hopes my balaclava would save me. Back in Ev's apartment, I had to work out where to go with what I knew.

CHAPTER 18

Visitors

The soft knock was too quiet. I didn't like that. My gun was out as I went towards the door, flattening myself against the wall first.

A good idea.

A double shotgun blast took out the door. Stopping to re-load before stepping in was a mistake by the shooter. I burst out through the hole, firing with a pistol at the shotgun freako, then added a spray around the hallway, at the other shadowy figures there.

None of the five bodies twitched.

I gathered up the guns. I had no real alternative but to ring Charlie.

"Yo."

"Caught Chico yet?"

"No."

"A bit of a mess on Evangeline's front door step. Don't know who they all are, but I can guess. San Franciscans. One nick-named "Lefty Four Eyes" – one hand missing, glasses (which explained why he'd taken so long to re-load the shotgun). I'm reasonably sure he – and possibly they - were with the Enforcer the night he shot that cop. Mates of Chico from prison days. He seems more and more to be tied in to all that as well. What this crew is doing on Evie's doormat I have not the slightest idea. Lots of shotguns and armaments. Need a special favour. Can your boys…er…clean up?"

"What the hell are you doing there?"

"Just picking up some personal things for Ev."

"Get out of there by the back door. Leave the guns."

"I'll lock them in the closet. I'm going to need to come into Langley again Charlie."

A day later, I sat opposite Charlie in his office at Langley. He was reading the report from his clean up crew. "That's a lot of heavy for a little old lady. They after you?"

"Don't know, don't care."

Charlie gave a heavy, dramatic sigh.

"Don't suppose you'll tell me where Evangeline is?"

"I told you - safe."

"You're a pain in the ass, d'Sousa."

"It doesn't make any sense to me. These guys are way off their base.

"Charlie. You gotta do some homework for me for once. This is **urgent** so don't just toss it in your out tray. It might explain the guys at Ev's flat.

"I know they were something to do with the Enforcer group. Five 'll get you ten, they were running with the Enforcer and Chico owes them big time. Get someone to bloody do some homework Charlie. And if you've still got a copy of that episode I brought, let's have a look and see what it's all about. Maybe he was pulling a fast one on the Marseilles mob himself.

"Meanwhile, I want you to know I listen to you. You reckoned it was strange those tunnels at Cherie's house were bricked up.

"Now what do you see in this photo?"

Charlie sighed and looked. "A cop talking into a radio."

"No Charlie, a lookout calling the coast is clear up and down the street for these." I showed pictures of the doors opening, of two trucks coming out.

"Everything is controlled by electronics. No-one is inside the warehouse except the drivers. Doors are opened by the press of a button – I'm guessing somewhere on the other side of those brick walls in Cherie's tunnels.

"Whilst I was watching inside, the old mechanics' pit opened up and two trucks drove out. The drivers went back inside so I was able to look more closely at the trucks. Sacks of flour."

"So?"

"Oh come off it, Charlie. Flour mills don't go to that extent to deliver their goods. You and I both know the trucks probably carried heroin. You and I both know there are three tunnels out of Cherie's place, which makes three possible exits to warehouses like this."

"Prove it."

"I can't. In fact, I'm not even sure they are there any more. They may just have borrowed the concept. Tell me, if you were bringing drugs into the US, how would you do it?"

"Through Chicago? By the Lakes."

"And if all your trucks were unloaded into a warehouse for customs, that had a bay like the one I saw?"

"You just take the two trucks loaded with bad stuff and away you go. Like I said – prove it."

"Like I said, I can't. Isn't that your bailiwick?"

"My **what?**"

"Isn't Homeland Security supposed to make sure nothing illegal creeps in – drugs, guns, butter, whatever?"

"Stop using fancy words, d'Sousa, I can't handle them right now. What makes you so sure the guys who arrived on your doorstep weren't connected with this? Probably saw you and followed you."

"No one sees and follows me. No, these guys were after someone else. I think it was Chico. Why on Ev's doorstep I don't know. Where the hell is that tape copy?"

Charlie sat in brooding silence 'til it came. We put it on.

Just as I should have gone to *Suspicion* earlier, it was clear I should have watched that damn tape from start to finish. It was mind-blowing.

The old episode of *Chicago* was the tale of our hero and his mates rounding up a gang of drug runners, who were using an old bootleggers' tunnel to import their goods. The reason the cast had used Ev and Brian's apartment – because it was just across the road from the old warehouse where the tunnel came up.

"No wonder Alan wanted to get his hands on that tape. I wonder what brought it to mind?"

"Let us say he almost certainly led the Marseilles gang there. He was and is the point of contact between everything." Charlie swung back in his chair, thinking.

"I'm taking this out of your hands, ***now*** Peggy. The D.E.A. can handle this however they want."

I held my hands up. "Hey, that's fine by me. Don't mention my name with the latest photos – just say they have come to your attention. Give them the ball and let them run with it."

He grunted. "Alright by you?"

"More than. You hired me to chase the Lone Wolf, not solve America's drug problems." I tiptoed to the door. It was clear Charlie's mind was running in all sorts of planning directions regarding the new information. If he heard me go, I would be surprised.

"Five," he said as I reached for the door handle.

"Beg pardon?"

"Five episodes of *Chicago* can be directly linked to cop killings. As for the mess you left us to clean up in Chicago...all in prison at the same time as Chico and the Enforcer. Any ideas?"

"I can imagine Chico boasting to cell mates: 'the real pot of gold sits in a little old lady's apartment in Chicago – it's worth a fortune'. With the publicity about Ev, they came for a look-see."

"Bloody hell!" Charlie swore.

I came back and sat down.

"That means it never occurred to you or any of your agents. Just for that, can one of your boys fly me back to New York?"

Charlie didn't need to know where Ev was just yet. Going to The Big Apple might put him off the scent. I could squeeze in a decent ballet or show. I figured I was due.

CHAPTER 19

Developments

I'd been standing opposite the San Francisco DAL branch of the bank for a week, having got there by a circuitous route in case Charlie's mates were following.

I'd become *au fait* with the regular bank people who came and went. I just wanted a sense of how the place worked.

Miriam was reclusive but even she ventured out on occasion. Alan's car was still parked in the underground parking area but there had been no sign of the man himself. The exercise was proving rather old, when a very spiffy out of town red Lamborghini roared in, parking next to his convertible.

Half an hour later, Alan emerged with a woman and the pair of them set off for lunch at what had become my favourite watering hole just a block away. Alan limped prodigiously. It gave me a deal of satisfaction knowing my peashooter was the cause.

The pair took a table, with the arrogant and ungracious manners of people who live to be seen and recognised, naturally near the window. It crossed my mind that sitting on display with Alan wasn't something I'd willingly do. Too many people wanted to kill him.

The *Maitre d'* smilingly found me a table in a slightly raised back area of the hostelry, discreetly dark, from where I could safely watch the goings on and enjoy a decent meal.

Alan's companion – had she been Australian – I would have pegged as a particular type. The tailored expensive power women's clothes screamed "lawyer" - not just a paid hack but a very senior legal. Her "out there on show" sort of attitude was of a person who would luxuriate in courtroom steps television interviews.

Here on the West Coast of the US? The clothes were probably New York. The lawyer, I concluded, was probably big time in Tinsel town. She had known where to find Alan (wanted murderer, drug dealer etc. that the law seemingly could not find), but above all he was an actor in a possible Oscar movie. That meant she represented seriously big money.

I dallied happily over a long lunch, as they chatted, when there was a sudden squeal of tyres followed by an extraordinary explosion.

The whole front window had gone. The lawyer lady just sat there, shocked, a stupid expression on her face, covered in glass. Alan must have dived at the sound of the tyres and hit the floor. He limped away without a backward look, without so much as a scratch, leaving his lawyer to pick up the pieces.

I slipped away before the police arrived and watched the front of DAL. Ms Legal came steaming down like an express train, slamming through the front door. I could hear shouting. The Lamborghini shot out of the car park with an excruciating change of gears.

Life in the fast lane, I figured, wasn't all it was cranked up to be.

Time to visit Ev and Mi and tell them the story to date of the "Old Pond".

CHAPTER 20

Boiling Point

Mi was flat-out busy downstairs. The time was coming when she would have to put the new manager in with some more staff. We did no more than wave, before I went upstairs to visit Ev, who was ensconced in her special chair watching her favourite soapie.

"Peggy! – now shush!"

I meandered out to the kitchen and made some coffee then stood in the doorway just evaluating Ev. She had come along in leaps and bounds. Her scars and bruising had disappeared. She was filling out slightly from Mi's good cooking and was starting to look genuinely healthy. It took years off her. Then I realised she'd also had a hair dye.

The music came up for the end of the serial and Ev clicked off the telly.

"I could do with some of that coffee," she said pertly, without so much as looking at me. I laughed.

"Getting sassy in your young age!"

I brought her a cup and refilled my own, sat down and told her the story.

"But," she spluttered, "That's what the episode with Brian was all about!"

"Yes, and that's why Chico went after it. All his years in prison, he was plotting, boasting he had a 'pot of gold' tucked safely in your apartment. Which explains some visitors I had."

I told her about the shotgun artists.

"Just as well I was on vacation when they called."

"What? What is just as well?" Mi had finally got free and came storming upstairs, filled with curiosity. I re-told the 'Old Pond' story, bringing it forward a little. That made Mi cross: "You came back to San Francisco and didn't come here at once?"

"Two things. I felt Charlie might be tailing me – I took the long way round, via New York. When I got here, I needed to see what was happening at the bank, if Alan was still there."

Mi couldn't get over how Alan was so easy to trace, yet the law didn't seem to be able to find him. I told them about the legal visitor and the shooting incident.

"I still say, I don't think the law is Chico's biggest worry. I would say there is so much stuff going on around him which **should** make him want to run to the law for cover. I hope I conveyed some of that to Miriam last time.

"The shotgun blast that took out the restaurant window must mean someone local is keeping an eye open for him. It had all the hallmarks of amateurs throwing together something at the last minute."

"But why are they after him- and who is 'they'?"

"Well, let's add it up. Obviously the Marseilles Gang have a grudge. With that tape in his possession he could have sent them a copy, threatening them with exposure. They may have decided to stop finessing and simply shoot him on sight. Frankly, I doubt this.

"His ex-con mates were the ones chasing him in Chicago. They ran with the Enforcer. But Chico strikes me as a man big on promises and small on delivery. He's also a druggie.

"Which means likely he owes someone local. Perhaps the balance of a hold up or some such, which he hasn't got around to splitting yet, because he's spent the money on drugs. These are all bad, mad guys who have spent more time in the big house than outside. Then, who knows…"

"What?"

"Maybe there's always a chance that the head of one of the best respected banks in the world is fed up with having a loose cannon for a brother-in-law and has put out a contract…despite Miriam."

Mi nodded gravely. "The restaurant window might well be explained that way."

Evie weighed in: "Chico sounds like one messed up individual."

"I personally think he's off the planet insane, perhaps he was always a genuine schizophrenic, protected by Miriam. In many ways, someone totally crazy might be inclined to be a such a dead shot – no fear or remorse… perfectly able to switch characters to a charming movie guy. The Lone Wolf might even be a "role" for his personality. He possibly began just as a cop who started off doing gangland contracts to satisfy his growing drug habit. One thing we now know for sure. There were no more Lone Wolf killings whilst he was in prison.

"Which is why when we nab him we must have hard evidence, like the Lone Wolf gun. I thought the gun must still be in Chicago, but Charlie says not – that they got a search warrant and found nothing in the apartment.

"He could, of course, have done what I did and simply dropped it into the Bay. I don't think so, if it's part of his persona.

"However, there is a better strand to follow."

"Which is?" Demanded Mi.

"He was almost certainly the guy who set up all those cop killings for the Enforcer. There is clear proof that in several towns where he was on location for his TV show and movies, working with the cops, driving around with them late at night and even wearing their uniforms - these are the places cops got hit by the Enforcer."

"He have inside knowledge which he pass on to the Enforcer?" Mi was incredulous. "Why?"

"I doubt for fun. The Enforcer could probably lay his hands on something Chico wanted."

"Drugs?"

"It always seems to come back to that. But why shoot his supplier in Chicago, Conseula?"

"Perhaps the sister promised more?"

Miriam was the key and I felt she would never talk. Instead I drove to LA to hunt out the pissed off lawyer.

CHAPTER 21

Los Angeles Makeover

Just turning up to a city the size of L.A. and looking for someone whose name I didn't know seems – shall we say – a little hopeful. But I had a plan. At the airport I hired a really cool sports job, that cost double the usual car hire, then booked into an uptown Hilton where the cars of my fellow guests already made mine look drab.

Then, following Mi's instructions, I took a tourist sight seeing bus and hopped off at China Town. I almost missed her LA book "shop" at first, since it resembled a super mart and took up half a block. I wandered through, going by degrees up and up and up, until I reached the offices and asked for Janet Jones.

Janet had the big corner office. I waved one of my own business cards. Even so, it took me three determined secretaries and a lot of time to get into her presence, since I'd arrived unannounced.

From a security point of view, I couldn't fault it. I figured by then they had the FBI file on me, besides knowing the inside size of my knickers.

Janet was a six foot three inch stunning San Franciscan Chinese, who looked like a super model. She had been a basketball point guard (whatever that was) for her elite college out East. Once getting her PhD in business she'd decided to knock around China and Hong Kong. According to Mi, Janet was an expert with any Chinese dialect going. She also held a black belt in Judo.

Mi had filched this treasure from Chan's bank, to open her L.A.

store. She was absolutely terrifying. She pondered my card, now in her hand. It was clear she was very unhappy.

"Ms. d'Sousa? I believe I may have heard Mi speak of you at some time?"

"Mi asked me to see you personally. We still aren't too sure who is listening in to phones just at the moment."

"Uhu."

"Things in San Francisco … er… need sorting a little after … um… some bother. I understand you also had a little trouble here." It seemed impolitic to go into fire bombings and the like. I felt, looking at Janet, I now understood why they were of little relevance.

"So you are not trying to sell us a security system?" That pretty face almost cracked a smile.

"Only if you feel you need it."

"Are you any good?"

"The best. Chan's banks, for instance…but let's get away from the sales pitch. Mi wanted me to assure you personally that only because of problems unrelated that have left the upstairs apartment unavailable, Mi would have turned the San Francisco office over to you weeks ago."

"Problems unrelated?" The unhappy Janet spat the words out.

"It's a long story. However, my further mission here is somewhat delicate. Mi was certain you could be of help."

"In what way?"

"I have to pass myself off tomorrow as a movie superstar. I need to dress accordingly. I didn't *actually* believe it until I met you, but she swears you have the best dress sense in the world…I always accused her of that."

Janet almost smiled, got up and strode around her desk, then around me. Then she clicked her fingers. "Of course! You're the famous Private Eye from Australia. No doubt on some top secret mission to save the world?" Her irony was huge.

"Let's just say, I'd prefer not to be known in this town as a private eye."

"Stand up," she ordered. "Twirl around." She laughed out loud. "It will cost and you will need to have something done with the hair…

by tomorrow, huh? Bloody typical. Mi usually wants things done by yesterday." She picked up her phone. "Cancel all my appointments for the rest of the day." Then she called her personal hairdresser and some other dress people.

"Hairdressing appointment at 3pm. You're lucky. Normally even real superstars need to book a week ahead in this town. We can shop and eat for the rest of the day."

I followed her to the private lift, which took us to the guarded car park where we got into her red Alfa Romeo and sped onto the nightmare that is L.A.'s tangled twist of motorways.

I thought as we drove I just didn't see this lunatic driver and supreme director tucked quietly into a few rooms above the store.

"Why San Francisco?" I asked.

She laughed. "Same old story. His name's Bill. Berkley Professor. Divorce not yet final. An apartment in Chinatown would be a good front as well as a pied-a-terre."

I breathed easier. "Makes sense…you didn't strike me as someone panting to live near her parents."

"Oh, you'd be surprised. That too. Need to keep an eye on them now they are getting on a bit. They'll never move. Seemed like a good idea all around. But Mi is dragging her feet…" She sighed and cut across three clear lanes at speed.

I hung on to the dashboard with all my strength. "I think Mi wants out of there too, especially as trade is picking up. We just have ourselves a situation."

"And let me guess. You are that situation." Janet sounded downright nasty.

"'Fraid so. On the plus side, Mi probably would not have gone ahead at this particular moment with the San Francisco store without my – er – need to be there."

"So I have you to thank?"

"In a roundabout way."

"I'll try and hold that thought." The Alfa had skipped off motorways and we were suddenly in an exclusive shopping zone. With frightening ease Janet flicked into a parking spot and took me to my fate.

The dresser had clicked unsympathetically at my burns from the car explosion (gosh, that seemed like a lifetime away). But these were now showing as red welts on my back and legs. "Don't stay so long in the solarium, Deary," he gushed, before hustling me through an amazing number of dresses in front of Janet, who gave the nod to three. Then we hit the shoe and accessories stores. Lunchtime, Janet led the way to a discreet restaurant with a stunning view, leaving our parcels locked in the Alfa boot. She finally deigned to talk. "You really don't care, do you?"

"Pardon me?"

"About clothes. You are an actress about to play a role, so you will dress for that role. Probably you will toss the clothes out afterwards." She was fascinated.

"Mi pointed out that I often need to dress down in my job, whilst she – and you – dress up. I suppose it's what one is comfortable with."

"Sometimes we choose the job to go with our clothes tastes." Janet remarked dryly.

I had to laugh. "I can't argue with that. However, it strikes me that sometimes so-called "Californian elegance" isn't …isn't…"

"Old world elegance?"

"Precisely. I need the strident tastes of Hollywood but don't know what they are."

After the hair appointment, at which I was streaked and made ragged in the latest 'in' style, Janet appeared at the door.

"Like it?"

"No, but that isn't the point."

The hairdresser threw his hands up as if insulted.

Janet placated him and I paid the bill.

"I never heard so much bullshit spoken in one day," I muttered as we drove back to my hotel.

"You don't like the clothes or your hair…"

"Don't worry, tomorrow, everyone will think I love both. Oscars should be handed out to private eyes, not super screen types."

"Tell me about it one day. Above all, tell Mi to hurry up and get her problems sorted."

"Thanks Janet. I really mean that. You've put yourself out for me in difficult circumstances."

She roared away in a car which would make my rented sports look ordinary…but it would have to do.

Now for the Studios.

CHAPTER 22

Peggy Goes To Hollywood

I got lucky. The Lamborghini showed after only three hours of waiting on day one. I'd found a nice shady possie close to the gates of the studio who presented *Suspense*. I'd watched the form of the guards as they pushed the barrier up checking ID's or issuing them to busloads of tourists.

Actors went through a different entrance, frequently photographed by the herds of tourists, often recognised, rarely waving their ID's around.

Dolled up as a superstar, it was time to go into action. Gunning my motor, I flashed in behind the Lamborghini, with the aplomb of someone about to be offered an Oscar.

"Hey, isn't that…??" I heard the milling tourists coo.

I waved back in turn, giving my best movie star smile. The guard at the gate also assumed I was 'someone' and made no effort to ID me.

I was in and tracking the lawyer lady's car. It wasn't too hard as I followed the road signs to the 'Executive Offices Only' section.

I squealed to a stop, parking dramatically, right next to the highly recognizable convertible Lamborghini that had burned rubber all the way from San Francisco - the lady lawyer's little toy.

Sarah Modesky (I learned her name as well as much other interesting information from rubbish in her car, whilst fitting a tracking device) eventually came hurtling out of the doors opposite, fired the Lamborghini up and shot out like a bullet.

I wasn't so slow off the mark, winking and nodding to the guards at the gate. My quarry was well out of sight even in those few seconds. That was OK, it suited my purpose. I flicked on the GPS tracker. Within half an hour we were barrelling down the coast road, where expensive houses were strung out alongside the Pacific Ocean. These were scenes right off postcards.

Modesky veered off sharply and I caught the flash of sun on chrome as large gates clanged shut behind her. I kept on driving to a beach café, parked and bought an ice cream, shucking my fancy gear for a pair of shorts, cool top and joggers.

A security nut, I could only shake my head at the row of mansions that like a Hollywood lot, were all ferocious front and no back, as I jogged past on the footpath that flowed back along the almost private beach towards Modesky's place. She was already lazing on the back porch, sipping something strong, long and cool in the heat. Importantly, she was alone.

"Hi! Ms. Modesky." I called out, clambering up the steps to her level, puffing. I took a mental deep breath as well. Things had been dragging on too long. I planned an 'end game'. Modesky, my gut feeling told me, was the absolute key.

"Do I know you?"

"I was in the restaurant the other day when someone took a pot-shot at Chico. Bad scene."

I sat down and proceeded to tell her about Chico, hardly pausing for breath as I spilled all I knew.

"So you see, he's wanted in Chicago for rape and murder, in San Francisco for cop murder. All that is standing between his arrest for raping an elderly friend of mine is the power and money of the studios."

"Very interesting, Miss er…"

"Chico must have given you the gun, or you know where it is. It wasn't in Chicago when the authorities searched and he didn't have it in San Francisco when he tried to shoot me the other day." (Nor, I'd made quite sure, was it the gun I'd found in her car.)

"I don't get why you are telling me this."

"You are an obvious – in fact – the only choice. Chico's victim in Chicago was a friend of mine. For that I promise you, he will go down, depend upon it. Let me tell you something else. His suppliers were the Marseilles boys."

"How cosmopolitan!"

"Think Triads, think Mafia. Very nasty, very violent.

"The woman Chico shot in a Chicago Shopping Centre was the daughter of Mitch Carpentier...the "godfather" of the Marseilles boys. They aren't supplying Chico any more. They figure he's a loose cannon. They have folded their tents and want the law to nab him. However, you personally are standing in the way. Be afraid, Ms. Modesky, be very afraid of sitting near Chico. The next bullet that comes may be for you."

"Fascinating!"

Now for the big hunch play.

"What should fascinate you most of all, Ms Modesky, is that you have taken possession of the gun that you **now** know killed many people **in this state**. That makes you an accessory. All this..." I waved my hand at the super-luxury beach house, "And yes, even the dear little Lamborghini, will certainly be history...if you aren't by then. Frankly Chico and you have more to worry about from his 'friends' than from the law in fifty something states...no matter how your employers control it.

"I'm offering you a deal. Turn the gun over to Homeland Security voluntarily and act like a concerned citizen...or take the consequences." I handed her a piece of paper with the words 'Homeland Security' and Charlie's phone number.

"I've heard some rubbish in my time, but this beats all." She pointed the piece of paper at me.

I played my ace. "If Chico is **your** personal supplier too, remember what I told you. Even the suppliers think he's a psycho. Get yourself a new supplier and do the good citizen act."

"Good-day Ms...?"

"Just remember, Ms. Modesky, I'm not about **justice**, I'm about **revenge**. Chico will go down, one way or the other, depend upon it."

I jogged away, hoping against hope that she would not pull a pistol from the revealing bathers she was wearing. Revealing because they not only showed a glorious body off to best advantage, but in the safety of her own home, showed she mainlined drugs, no matter how carelessly she had flicked a towel over her legs. The sad news was that one way or the other, Ms. Modesky would be dead too soon. The good news – she hadn't shredded that piece of paper in my face.

Back at the car, hot and sweaty, I decided I was much in need of another ice cream. I heard rather than saw the Lamborghini roar past on the main highway. It was headed for San Francisco.

I wasn't planning to go anywhere for a few days. I had enough information on Modesky to dig up some dirt. Knowing she had left town, it might be a good time to drop in at night and check out Villa Modesky for myself.

Back at the hotel, an invitation was waiting for me at the desk. The Australians in Hollywood were having an A-list bash for an upcoming film. I'd heard about it earlier and thought my expensive new rags might come in useful for something, so I'd phoned Zac Turner, my old director mate, to see if he could swing an invite. He'd come through.

I stepped from the cab onto the red carpet.

"Darls, you never fail to amaze me!" The voice came from Lowell, who had just emerged from the limo behind.

"Where's Oscar nominated girlfriend tonight?" I teased.

"Just got back from promoting the film in Oz. Says she's seen and heard enough Australians to last her a lifetime!" He gave a bit of a sad shrug.

"Hope that doesn't mean she's throwing you over?"

"Easy come, easy go, Darls. Now, may I escort you down the red carpet?" So he did, to much flash photography. We even made the Social Pages the next day – naming me and suggesting I was about to make the move from behind to the front of the cameras.

I got a phone call from Janet about the social pages picture. "My dress and hairstyle looked superb, don't you think?"

I could only laugh at how careful she was not to flatter me. "I have to agree, they did."

"And are you joining us in Tinsel Town as is suggested?"

"Hollywood couldn't afford me…I don't come cheap."

"Uhu. How's the 'situation' going?"

"Definitely progressing. Incidentally, do you know anything about a Sarah Modesky?"

"Tinsel Town's Ms. Fixit? We shared rooms and boyfriends back East in college a hundred years ago. Brilliant scholar but has gone to the dark side of the law. Says it keeps her in Lamborghinis. More like most of what she earns goes up her nose," she snorted sarcastically.

"She got a regular feller?"

"Been seen around some with some movie star guy – Chico something."

"She originally from San Francisco too?"

"No. Comes from a long line of discreet and very dull Boston Judges. Not her style. Bright lights and all that for her."

"Interesting. Thanks again Janet for all the help."

"Yeah."

CHAPTER 23

Unilateral Strike

I examined Chateau Modesky carefully from the outside on the way home. Approachable as it had been from the beach with its owner home, I betted it was a different story given the high gates out front. A touch of a button almost certainly brought down steel shutters on the veranda on the ocean side.

So I cruised by a few times, checking for cameras, alarms and other problems. A Rottweiler snarled at me through the main gates. I dislike boofers intensely. OK, so I'm afraid of the very large ones with teeth and attitude.

I returned at night, sprayed the camera, climbed the fence and tasered the boofers – both of them – hoping there were no more sleeping.

Getting into the mansion house was child's play after that. I was right about the steel shutters, which were good for me, as I could put the lights full on.

I didn't discover **the** gun – the one thing I was looking for – but carefully combing through Sarah's private safes (I found 3), not only was there an enormous amount of cash money, but there were lists of people. Some I recognised as well-known film stars. Some were ones who had bought drugs off Chico and Babe in Cannes. I took photos of the lists.

I didn't find a passport. Perhaps she took as much cash as she could carry and ran.

It suggested also that Ms. Tinsel Town did a strong racket in blackmailing stars in order to pay for her own habit and yes, little trinkets like the car and so on.

After a couple of trials, I flicked the lights off, pressed the up button on the steel shutters, got into position then pressed the down button.

I easily rolled clear and onto the beach track.

I was back to my car with some useful internal photos within the hour and back in San Francisco before daybreak.

I immediately sent the photos off to Charlie and tried to sleep off Tinsel Town. Being over-tired I just couldn't fall off to dreamland, so I pulled out the computer, updated it and even checked out the papers on the net. The headline jumped out at me: *Australian Explosion caused by San Francisco Terrorists.*

I immediately flicked to my hometown paper, gasping with relief as I realized it could only be a file picture of Lowell on the front page, cleverly juxtaposed with the charred mess on Fremantle wharf. Sifting through hundreds of sensationalised stories I managed to distil the essential facts.

Firstly, from the captain of *SF Express,* which had left San Francisco, successfully negotiated a choppy Pacific to Japan, going on to make its exchange of cargo in Shanghai, where it had picked up the maximum load of containers of tiles for the insatiable building trade. The heavily laden vessel veered out to sea to avoid two cyclones headed from Indonesia down the West Coast of Australia. As a result, the *SF Express* docked three days late at Fremantle port.

The container ship was unloaded that night. Midnight found the gates locked on a wharf that had earlier been a scene of frenzied activity. Crane drivers had long since gone. The mountains of unloaded containers had been plucked one by one and driven off by massive road trains.

All that remained on the quiet, darkened wharf was a small pile of containers marked for delivery to the Fremantle area.

Suddenly, one of the containers exploded. Its metal shot out like shrapnel into the containers around. Its doors blew off, smoke and flames pouring out. The echoing explosion was heard half way to Perth on a balmy summer night.

Fearing terrorists, the police, fire brigade, customs and security picked quickly over the whole mess, becoming certain of some facts. Based on information supplied by Captain Rashid, it was rapidly established that the explosion had come from within a container of special antiques and arts addressed to Lowell Hanwright's warehouse, loaded in San Francisco. The explosives were thought to be on a timing device.

A furious Rashid had raged to the press that had the weather been worse, to make the ship been even a day later, it would have blown the bottom off the *SF Express* which would have gone straight to the floor of the Indian Ocean taking him and his whole crew with it.

Had the container been delivered on time to Lowell's warehouse, the explosion and subsequent fireball would have reduced that famous massive warehouse filled with antiques to ruin and killed everyone inside.

However, left snuggled between containers of tiles on an empty wharf, the explosion had been neutralised safely.

Luck.

Forensics had already been to work. They felt that a very large quantity of plastic explosive had been wrapped around something tucked at the back of the container – like a painting – now destroyed. However, the remains of a crude and amateur timer had been discovered. The manifest had shown a painting addressed to Peggy d'Sousa from DAL galleries was the likely culprit.

To settle the locals, the Police Commissioner had quickly announced that it was NOT a terrorist strike, but something aimed at Lowell's own firm, confirming the suspect party in the US was already under the scrutiny of one Charlie Deakins of Homeland Security.

I was stunned. Charlie's name wouldn't have been there without his express permission. He hadn't rung me. The explosion had happened even as Lowell and I walked the red carpet in Tinsel Town.

I didn't doubt that Lowell – my dearest friend for many years – was the actual target of the madman now holed up in DAL's Gallery.

This had to stop. It had to stop now.

CHAPTER 24

San Francisco Blues

I arrived opposite DAL at daybreak. Tucked under my coat was a very big gun. I didn't know what to do and shrank into my normal corner, trying to come up with a plan. I was amazed to see Lowell come storming past and disappear into the Gallery.

There was an awful lot of shouting going on.

I snuck in just in time to get the gist. Lowell was ticking off what could have happened if…and if and if…

Chico put in an appearance.

Miriam turned to him.

"Tell Lowell it's all nonsense!" she shouted.

"Oh, you liked my little present?" He jeered. "Bet there wasn't much left of your friend's painting or your stupid antiques business!"

He laughed a crazy laugh and twiddled a gun. Furious, Lowell ignored the gun and absolutely pasted him with a left hook. Chico went down like a sack of potatoes, then raised the gun to shoot Lowell.

I pulled out my shotgun and yelled: "Don't even think about it, Chico! I promise I'll use this."

"Hold it! Just hold it right there!" Miriam was screaming, out of control. She was also pointing **the gun** at me. Everyone froze in a three way Mexican standoff.

"Get the hell out of my gallery and my life, d'Sousa!"

I stood very still until Lowell had retreated, watching Chico's trigger finger all the time. Once Lowell was safe, I backed out the door to a waiting Lowell.

"You wouldn't have used that thing?"

"Couldn't have him shoot you, old son."

"Quite."

I rang Charlie. "The gun is definitely back in San Francisco DAL."

"I **KNOW,** d'Sousa. I had a call from a Sarah Modesky. Said she would turn state's witness. I agreed to a deal if she returned the gun to its owner.

"Now clear the hell out of there or you'll get caught in the crossfire. My sniper team has you in its sights and says you are waving a shotgun."

"But…"

"Put it on the ground…and *back away fast!*"

I did and Lowell and I backed off as some space age dressed characters brushed past us and into the gallery. I stayed online.

"Got the gun," Charlie reported, hobbling out of a nearby doorway.

"Tell them to be careful, Chico's armed."

He cursed. There was a shot, then a volley of shots in reply.

Charlie ducked inside then reported back. "Winged Lola, but not seriously. Chico bought the farm."

"You aren't supposed to be on active duty!"

"And you aren't supposed to be toting a shotgun without a licence. Give it to me before somebody gets hurt!"

Miriam was brought out first, weeping.

"Take her back to New York, Hanwright then put her on a plane for Italy. Make sure she gets on. She'll only complicate the case. I like tidy ends." He waved up a dark saloon car that came out of nowhere and hustled them both away discreetly.

I sat down on the pavement and waited as ambulances now tore into view. One took a body bag. The other the bleeding sniper Lola accompanied by Charlie. As police forensics turned up, the other space-age snipers slipped quietly away. I heard a helicopter in the distance.

Everyone ignored me. I was alone on the gallery steps when Charlie came back an hour later.

"Lola?"

"She's fine."

"I hear she's one of Charlie's Angels?"

"Now don't you start. Yes, they are all women, and for the record, the best snipers in the service. Tell me about Chico's broken jaw?"

"Must have fallen badly."

Later that night I took Charlie to see Evangeline. He whistled, as he explored the little setup above the bookshop and all the security with the ferocious Hong Kong boys. "No wonder you're the highest paid security gal in the world, Peggs. Remind me to hire you sometime!"

We had to wake Evie.

"It's over, Evie. Chico is dead. There won't be a trial. We'll just need a statement from you eventually."

"I can go home?"

I nodded.

"Nothing against San Francisco – I just miss home." The old lady sighed happily and went back to sleep.

Charlie and I snuggled on the couch in the living room, watching the TV news as a heavily uniformed and braided Superintendent Clarke claimed credit for all that had passed.

"Why did you hit on Modesky?" Charlie eventually asked.

"It made sense. When I told her things about Chico I suspect she'd arrived at the same conclusion. I was offering her an out."

"With the explosion in Fremantle, then her singing, I had no trouble getting judges' signatures to search the bank. I told Modesky to make sure the gun was there when I did."

"I hope she gave you names of suppliers for all that."

"We did OK. She comes out looking good. Keeps her job at the studios. The movie can still get the Oscar. Probably do better now with that sort of crowd pull over Chico. Now, about that shotgun…"

"I liberated it from Ms. Modesky's car boot a few days ago, rather than be on the business end of it."

He whistled. "Probably figured her insurance was gone. Pushed her into ringing me. Good move."

"Well I'm damned, did I hear right? Charlie actually thanked me for bringing the Lone Wolf to book, nailing the cop murderers behind the Enforcer, cleaning up the drug scene of Hollywood – not to mention Chicago. Incidentally, what news from Chicago?"

"The D.E.A. only found and followed two tunnels from the warehouse. Both were crammed end to end with lorries, loaded with heroin. Came to an end at brick walls. Broke them down and found themselves in Cherie's cellar. They broke down the other brick wall and followed it all the way to the docks. Same MO as the warehouse opposite Evangeline…a pit that opened up. They are watching it."

"Good luck to them. Cherie is long gone. Once they emptied the cellars and bricked up the walls, they had moved on. Why do you suppose they killed Conseula?"

"Payback. You of all people should know what crime fathers do to daughters who don't play the game."

I let that go with a shudder. Charlie held me a little tighter. "When will Evangeline get due credit and MONEY for her services in cracking that absolutely monster Chicago drug ring?"

"Can't go public just yet…but…"

"But some money could start drifting her way soon? She isn't getting any younger. She's had a bad time…"

"See what I can do."

"You're an ok-guy Mr Deakins. I look forward to your ribs mending."

CHAPTER 25

Antique Heaven

Famous for great music festivals, Newport was rapidly becoming the centre of where it was at for American antiques.

I knew it was big. How big, I did not understand until I fulfilled my bargain and turned up to support it – although why the place needed an extra soul who didn't give a fig about antiques was utterly beyond me.

Yet it was a time to relax. Janet had been settled in the new China Town bookstore with complete explanation, and although the Alfa was a tight fit down the side, she never seemed to have a problem.

The "painted lady" had been reluctantly returned to its owners (without any explanations), in surprisingly good shape.

Miriam had retreated to Italy and had taken up painting again – perhaps because of her angst, the results would satisfy even her.

Evie had been returned to her beloved Chicago and a "talk" software set up on which she had become something of a terrorist, but at least her 'boys' had constant contact and could keep an eye out for her.

Footloose and fancy free, I had no excuse than to present myself to the Newport Antiques fair.

I waved to Lowell. There was no chance of getting close enough to chat, he was so surrounded by acolytes. Soon the auction would begin.

He managed to slip next to me as the hammer began to fall on some major items. Let me tell you, ladies and gentlemen, we are talking serious money for junk here.

Then the auctioneer carefully held aloft a pot, claimed to be very early American Indian, likely over a thousand years old. The crowd was hushed. This was the Big Ticket item of the day.

Before the auctioneer could place it down to start the bidding, the pot disintegrated in his hand, smashed by an arrow that went on and with amazing accuracy (or sheer bad luck), struck the auctioneer in the heart.

I was already moving fast towards the probable direction of the shooter....but that is another story...

The End